Bringing
HOPE

One Police Officer's Journey
With Empathy on the Path to Service

Bringing
HOPE

One Police Officer's Journey
With Empathy on the Path to Service

LORENZO ORTIZ

Bringing Hope:
One Police Officer's Journey With Empathy on the Path to Service

Jones Media Publishing
10645 N. Tatum Blvd. Ste. 200-166
Phoenix, AZ 85028
JonesMediaPublishing.com

12 11 10 9 8 7 6 5 4 3 2 1

Printed in the United States of America

ISBN: 978-1-948382-82-3 (paperback)

To my inspirations, Enzo and Olivia. You are my Why.
Love you both until the end of time.

CONTENTS

PREFACE

Bringing Hope is a creative work born from the sacrifices, passions, and deep emotions amassed during my career as a law enforcement officer, learning from others, making mistakes and being very patient with the process. While I penned these ideas to paper, I am not the mind behind the lessons shared here. Visionaries such as Carl Rogers and Dr. Robert Cialdini are pioneers in their respective fields, influencing many of the ideas and communication tactics exemplified in this parable.

However, the true credit goes to the women and men of law enforcement who put their bodies, hearts, and minds in jeopardy to provide peaceful alternatives to those engulfed in the darkest moments of their lives. This tale is a tribute to those people who have chosen to don the badge, being the kind of officer they'd want around on their loved ones' toughest days.

Thank you to my friends and colleagues who've helped me to learn, thrive, and help people along the way. You've made a difference in countless lives. I love you all and would ride the wave with you again in a heartbeat. Thank you to all of you who continue to fight the good fight, making the priority of life your highest priority. And don't forget to bring hope!

***This is a work of fiction. Any names or characters, businesses or places, events or incidents, are fictitious. Any resemblance to actual persons, living or dead, or actual events is purely coincidental.

FOREWORD

With more than 21 years as a crisis negotiator in one of the nation's largest cities, I played a role in over 400 hostage, crisis, barricade, and suicidal incidents, serving as a team member or leading the crisis negotiations team within the Special Assignments Unit.

As a negotiator, I plunged into the heart of human crisis. Facing hostage situations and frantic calls, I navigated through some of life's most harrowing moments, not just for myself, but for those caught in the chaos. My role was to guide them through the storm, helping them find their own path to safety, even amidst the most turbulent emotions.

Effective communication demands skill, but crisis communication transcends to an art form—a profound set of skills essential for maneuvering through the intricacies of human emotion by attentively listening and comprehending motivations. Very few truly understand what a crisis negotiator's job is; valuable lessons from these professionals could enhance communication skills for police officers, from patrol to command staff. Responding to a crisis can bring stress and chaos upon any officer charged with the task of communication as well as the subject suffering that day. A crisis negotiator should strive to possess and embody the qualities of empathy, good listening, calm demeanor, patience, and a team mindset (just to name a few) when dealing with these life-altering situations.

As you read "Bringing Hope," the book will walk you through the story of 'Tony' and the strategies he and his peers use to help people. The officers in this story work under the pressure of the most intense incidents utilizing empathy, understanding, de-escalation techniques and an unwavering commitment to the preservation of life amidst the chaos of crisis. You will also see how 'Tony' adopted lessons from his triumphs, mistakes, and tragedies to better serve his community. We share these stories with the hope that officers will find inspiration to bring light to the darkness, offering glimmers of hope to those in despair.

— Jan Dubina
Negotiator/Team Lead Special Assignments Unit,
Phoenix Police Department (Retired)

INTRODUCTION

"Jim, my name is Tony. I am here to help you come out of this situation safely," said Tony. Speaking into the cell phone, his voice remained calm as he peered through the thick ballistic windshield of the armored vehicle.

From his vantage point, Tony could see the suspect on the other end of that phone call, sitting with a black semi-automatic pistol in his right hand, held to his right temple. Jim looked as nervous as any person possibly could be. Sweating profusely, his eyes bulged as he scanned his surroundings, responding to all the commotion as the swarm of officers took their positions.

According to the drug investigators who initiated this investigation and subsequent chase, Jim had shown up at a truck stop where they were surveilling known drug dealers. He acted suspiciously, repeatedly driving by their investigation area in the same Cadillac now surrounded by police Tahoes. When the investigators attempted to approach Jim, he accelerated, peeling out of the parking lot, fleeing as if he had just committed an armed robbery.

The investigators sensed trouble brewing, a feeling that intensified when Jim recklessly plowed into a passerby on a bicycle while hastily escaping the parking lot. To add to their concern, Jim brandished the black pistol he currently held, waving it out of the window and menacingly pointing it at both officers and the countless citizens strolling through the expansive truck stop parking lot. Unbeknownst to Jim, his panicked attempt to deter officers from chasing him inadvertently provided them with sufficient grounds, according to their policy, to initiate pursuit of his Cadillac. As one officer stood by with the injured bicyclist and waited for the fire department to arrive, the rest of the officers gave chase.

A Patrol Lieutenant cleared over the radio with the magic words, "Pursuit is authorized."

As Jim took off down the road, the Cadillac weaving in and out of traffic, the unmarked vehicles chasing him gave way to the fully marked Tahoe's of the patrol officers who took up the pursuit. Little did Jim know the agency's air unit and S.W.A.T. team had also heard the radio traffic signal and were now en route to the commotion. Jim, channeling his best Fast and Furious stunt, maneuvered through traffic with daredevil swerves, inches away from other vehicles. Ignoring traffic lights, he aimed to outstrip the marked police vehicles in pursuit, their lights flashing, and sirens wailing as the chaotic chase unfolded. Just as Jim looked in his rear view for the hundredth time, he saw the marked vehicles backing off. Thinking he had bested the officers with his slick driving brought a wry smile to Jim's face.

That's when Jim caught the rhythmic 'whoomp, whoomp, whoomp' of the police helicopter hovering above him. His heart raced, and he became acutely aware of his profuse perspiration, his shirt now drenched and chilling. Struggling to locate the helicopter, Jim overlooked that he had unwittingly entered a construction zone. The change in traction beneath his tires hit him as the Cadillac came to an abrupt stop, propelling him into the steering wheel of the late-model car – after all, bad guys are notorious for skipping seatbelts. Jim slammed his right foot on the gas pedal, only to find the tires spinning and throwing up gravel in vain. The Cadillac had become wedged on debris left by workers, causing a surge of real panic for Jim.

His vision started to narrow, blacking out his peripheral view and time started to slow down for him as he watched marked and unmarked police units surround him. Jim's breathing was quickening and shallowing with every breath and he felt terror, almost as if having an out of body experience. Seeing officers in full blue uniforms and some in tactical uniforms as they exited their vehicles in haste, he felt like they were moving so much faster than him. The officers were taking up positions with handguns drawn, rifles slung and some weapons he had never seen before. Jim's first instinct was to grab the black pistol from the passenger seat and raise it to his head.

Jim pressed the gun to his temple forcefully, then yelled out, "Come any closer and I'll blow my fucking head off!"

Antonio, better known to his colleagues as Tony, and his partner, Monica, found themselves in the perfect location when the call crackled over the hot channel that morning. It was important for them to remain centralized in the city during their shift rather than being confined to an office. Their police vehicle was their office. That morning, as Tony and Monica were leaving a convenience store on the south side, Drug Enforcement Unit officers requested assistance on the hot channel with a man barricaded in his own car. The suspect was threatening suicide, and the scene was unfolding tactically. Tony and Monica carefully proceeded to the area of the incident, paying close attention to the radio traffic to determine which would be the safest area to respond from.

As Tony arrived, the S.W.A.T. armored vehicles pulled up simultaneously. This opportune moment allowed Tony and Monica to swiftly board the armor before it reached the suspect's car. This way, they avoided the need for a later escort into the armor with a ballistic shield by S.W.A.T. officers. Tony parked on a sidewalk and, as he was exiting the vehicle, Monica was quick to remind him to grab their gas masks from the back of the Tahoe, just in case any chemical munitions were used by the tactical team. They had learned from a couple forgetful instances that not having a gas mask could make for a painful and rather 'spicy' stint in the armored vehicle.

S.W.A.T. officers, arriving in their substantial equipment trucks, took over from the Drug Enforcement detectives and patrol officers who had initially established a perimeter around the suspect's Cadillac. The patrol officers effectively secured the area, preventing civilian vehicles from entering, but a crowd of pedestrians with cell phones out, recording the action, remained in the vicinity.

The armored vehicle, a giant gray tank-looking truck, pulled into the scene. Tony and Monica identified the armored vehicle's driver as Bryan, a familiar face from numerous calls akin to the current situation. They signaled Bryan, knowing he was exceptionally vigilant when approaching scenes, and he reciprocated the signal. Bryan decelerated sufficiently for them to swing open the heavy door of the armor and join him in the back. After exchanging brief greetings, Bryan handed Tony the microphone for the public announcement speaker on the armored vehicle, bringing it to a halt right in front of the Cadillac.

"Thank you," said Tony, and at that moment, the same heavy door through which they had entered the armored vehicle swung open.

Sergeant Marsh was standing in front of the open door and hollered in, "Get some quick intel on this guy from Drug Enforcement and start doing your thing!"

Sergeant Marsh was heavily respected; he'd proven himself over the years as a S.W.A.T. supervisor and operator. Sergeant Marsh always showed great respect for his responding negotiators and today was no different. He just needed them to get to work.

Monica, trying to be a team player, hopped out of the armored vehicle to get a basic story from the other investigators. Before Tony could start on the P.A. system, someone outside the armor asked for his cell phone number. As Monica transmitted their phone number over the radio, someone relayed it to Jim through the P.A. system of one of the patrol Tahoes. Time seemed to crawl for Tony as he waited for the phone to ring.

Sergeant Marsh yelled into the armor, "Are we on the line yet?!"

Tony started to yell back to Sergeant Marsh when the cell phone on his lap began to ring. Tony answered, but the call immediately dropped. Now, Tony began to feel anxious but he took a deep breath and called the number back immediately. No answer, straight to voicemail. He called again, no answer. Tony began to worry. He wondered if they had lost their one opportunity to speak with Jim.

Just then, Tony's phone rang and he answered. "Jim, my name is Tony. I am here to help you come out of this situation safely."

Tony, drawing on years of experience, acknowledging past mistakes, benefiting from mentorship and extensive training, was aware that his first impression would shape the entire interaction. Therefore, he remained calm, showed no sign of judgment, and ensured he conveyed a genuinely caring tone. As the negotiation continued, there were ups and downs with all the stress and emotion Jim had going on. Despite the challenges, Tony, clear on his mission, persevered with Monica's support. Eventually Jim went from a highly emotional, demanding, suicidal suspect in a car who was facing an 80-year sentence for a parole violation, to a guy who knew he'd made a lot of bad decisions and just wanted to say goodbye to his girlfriend before he went into custody that day.

As Tony got Jim to peacefully surrender to the tactical officers, he couldn't help but feel a little sorry for Jim. Tony had learned the hard way that, for negotiators who care deeply about what they do, this can be a tough side effect of approaching suspects with empathy. As Tony was working through that feeling, he also knew he and Monica had played a big role in bringing the incident to a peaceful resolution for Jim and the officers on scene. Tony took that as a reassuring thought and was thankful none of his fellow officers had to use deadly force. Tony would later learn that Jim was using a fake gun during the incident, making him even more grateful that none of the officers had taken Jim's life that day.

CHAPTER 1

THE FOUNDATION

Tony was born Antonio Mendoza to an immigrant family in Tucson, Arizona. Tony went by Antonio all throughout his school years, maintaining this name until he was around 36 years old, right in the midst of his police career. Tony was always proud of his roots, but growing up he often felt torn between two worlds. His parents had him enrolled in schools where he stood out as one of very few Latino students, forcing Tony to learn how to adjust to different worlds very early on in life. When most people envision an immigrant Mexican family, they might imagine laborers of some kind. Tony's family had been fortunate in Mexico, and his mother was able to come to the United States when she was a small girl. She grew up in the U.S. and would eventually go on to be a clerk of the county courts. Tony's father, Antonio Sr., also grew up in Mexico but didn't move to the United States until he was in his early 20's.

Antonio Sr.'s home life wasn't terrible, but it wasn't a particularly affectionate home either. This made it easier for him to leave home at an early age and go off to military school. In a very real sense, he never came back home after that. Antonio Sr. always made it a priority to take care of his mother after his father passed away from emphysema—but there always remained a sense of distance between Antonio Sr. and his mother. Tony would later observe this frigid relationship between his grandmother and Antonio Sr. over the years. One thing Tony always did see was that his dad worked harder than anyone he knew, ensuring the family had a comfortable home, nice things, and delicious traditional Mexican food on the table.

Meanwhile, Tony's mother grew up in the United States, in a border town. Tony's maternal grandmother was very loving, but tensions were high in their home because of Tony's severely alcoholic grandfather who left the family in poverty because of his addiction. As a family, they always worried what a knock at the door would bring, since Tony's grandfather was always out in public drinking somewhere. Tony's mother had a strained relationship with her siblings as well as her own mother who passed away when Tony was only 9 years old. As Tony aged, he began to believe his mother really struggled in many ways because of her hellacious upbringing. Tony would later realize that his mother really didn't know what a peaceful home looked like.

Tony's parents first met at a social event while Antonio Sr. was in college in Mexico. Antonio Sr. had studied architecture and was forced to complete his studies in the U.S. due to strikes at the Mexican University he was attending. Tony's parents' bond grew stronger as Antonio Sr. continued in his architecture program at an American University he had been accepted to as an international student. They were married shortly after Antonio Sr. had obtained his bachelor's degree and started in the architecture field with a large firm. Tony's maternal aunt, who he called 'tía', played a major role in his childhood and lived with the family when he was young as a help to Tony's parents.

With both Tony's parents having good steady jobs, they were able to send Tony to a private Catholic school, where academic discipline was a must. This hard-learned discipline would later be something Tony would see as a blessing. It took a lot for Tony's parents to afford sending him and his sister to private school, but it would later pay off. Tony faced difficulties growing up, feeling like an outsider in wealthier environments. Despite not being the top student in his classes, he worked hard and did well, learning valuable lessons along the way.

In high school, Tony joined the football team after coaches noticed his size when he was a freshman. Throughout the years, he consistently held starting positions as an offensive and defensive lineman. However, Tony was aware that playing college football wasn't in his future. Recognizing this, Antonio Sr. took the initiative to encourage Tony to develop educational plans for his life after high school. This seemingly small act of discipline and foresight would eventually prove pivotal in shaping Tony's professional success.

As Tony finished high school, he had no real idea of what he wanted to do, but figured he would make some decisions along the way. Tony had developed a 'go with the flow' way about him as a teen. It wasn't a bad thing, but he just didn't have a passion to follow yet. Tony's mother pushed him to take the medical school route, always saying he had the "hands of a healer." Tony, knowing his mother, believed she really wanted him to be a physician because of the clout it would bring the family. Trying to be the good son, Tony started down that career path even though he really wasn't that interested. In his first two years of undergrad, Tony enrolled in pre-med classes and activities, but he never really found joy or passion in those sciences. The absence of enthusiasm made school that much more of a grind. Classes felt like so much more work as the semesters creeped by. Tony had picked up a student job at a lab in the university hospital as a research assistant. He watched how miserable and stressed the medical students looked and he just couldn't see himself working that hard to feel and look so dejected all the time. Eventually, Tony began looking for an opportunity to leave the pre-med field.

Tony had met a lot of acquaintances through his classes at the university and, in April of his sophomore year, some of those people invited him to work in a program called New Start. Tony had actually been through the New Start program the summer after his senior year of high school. The program was an introductory summer school for new students to experience campus and classes before the start of freshman year. Tony recalled having so much fun during his participation in New Start. The program was designed for students to enroll in one introductory-level university class, paired with an elective that aimed to equip them for sustained success at the college level. Tony attributed this program and his very challenging high school education to his success in his university classes. He thought, why not contribute to a program that he knew had positively impacted so many individuals.

In mid-April, Tony showed up for the New Start information session and it seemed like a great summer gig to make a little extra money and pay it forward to others coming into the university. One of the major influences New Start had on Tony's career came from the retreat he'd attended as part of the program preparation. As summer heated up in the desert, the conference took the group of student advisors out to a rural area in the hills of Arizona, where it was ten degrees cooler than the city. The retreat was fantastic, and it wasn't just because of the temperature change and beautiful scenery.

This group of student advisors were a fun and outgoing group who stayed up until all hours of the night playing card games, talking, and listening to music. No alcohol, no drugs, just young adults having a really nice time together. Tony felt like he'd found his people. During the initial full day of the retreat, Tony listened to the expectations and responsibilities assigned to them as student advisors, along with the program's rules. The morning was lengthy, but the facility provided a delicious catered lunch.

As the group of future student advisors sat down after lunch, the speaker introduced himself as Randy, the program's director. He joked with the group, trying to keep the after-lunch session light as he spoke on the topic of active listening. As many of the student advisors slipped into a stupor that most presenters expect after a good meal, Tony felt as if he had been electrified (in a good way, not like a taser). As Randy went on about "minimal encouragers, paraphrasing and mirroring," Tony couldn't help but feel drawn to the topic in a way he wouldn't come to fully understand until almost 20 years later. Tony just knew that this topic spoke to him, and he really liked the material. That day, Tony made a few notes with the intention of applying them as a student advisor. The most crucial insights he gained from the session included:

1. Communication isn't the same as talking.
2. People need and crave respect.
3. If people need to talk, make the time to speak with them.
4. If you are genuine, you will gain influence with people.
5. It's not so much what you say, it's how you say it.

Tony loved helping people, especially helping new students have a positive experience their first year of college. Every day he came into work at the program feeling alive and energized. One particularly amazing day was move-in-day. Tony didn't know why, but he just felt so awesome helping the freshman and their families move into their new dorm rooms. Tony smiled huge as he carried bags and small furniture up the stairs of the dorm, all the while making conversation with the arriving families.

At one point, the program organizer said to Tony, "You are having way too much fun with this man!" Tony observed that many students appeared nervous and didn't engage in much conversation that day. However, recalling the advice from the program retreat presentation, he understood that his positive energy and smile would have a greater impact on the freshmen than his words. By the end of the day, Tony felt a deep sense of fulfillment, with numerous parents and students openly expressing gratitude for the assistance provided by the advisors. Tony knew that this day would be etched in his memory for a long time.

Tony considered the program a success, and he willingly volunteered a significant amount of his time, despite not receiving compensation for the extra hours he dedicated to assisting. Another part of the program Tony loved was instructing a one-hour block, once a week, giving students tips on how to succeed in their first year. The students in the class were very receptive and, although Tony had been super nervous, he started to develop an enjoyment for instructing. Tony found this ironic, as he remembered how nervous he would get in school any time he was forced to speak in front of his peers.

The number one lesson he took away from instructing that summer was that he just needed to really learn the material he was presenting; the more comfortable he became with the material, the simpler it became to speak about it with passion. Tony even focused some of his instruction on topics he learned from the pre-program retreat, and similar topics, which made him appreciate the science of communication even more.

As the program wound down that summer, Tony was sad but knew he had his own studies to get back to. He felt lackluster going into the semester. One downside of Tony's experience with the summer program was that he ended his relationship with the girl he had been dating since his senior year in high school. She had complained about how much time Tony was putting into the program, and it eventually led to their parting ways. It was upsetting, but he also knew they were both ready for change and it was going to be a stressful year for him anyway. He still had a lab job at the university hospital and a steady flow of science and math classes that would be taking up a lot of his time.

As the school year began, a fellow New Start advisor mentioned another program to Tony that she believed he might really like and be well-suited for. The program was called Advanced Preparation for Excellence. It was similar to New Start in that it helped prepare young junior high and high school students for a college experience. The program was time-consuming, requiring weekly sessions at a junior high school and a high school to instruct teens on college preparation and achieving success in high school.

It sounded like an amazing opportunity to Tony and another way to continue on the path that New Start had forged for him. He went to an information session about the Academic Preparation for Excellence program and never looked back. Tony would soon put in his two-week notice at the laboratory and, as he delved into the world of education and higher education advocacy, Tony would change his university major to Psychology—another game changer. Unaware at the time, these choices would ultimately guide him towards a successful journey lasting numerous years, albeit through indirect means.

CHAPTER 2

THE TRANSITION

The years zoomed by and Tony kept on his educational path with lots of learning and plenty of mistakes—both professional and personal. Graduation had come and gone and, with no real next step, Tony found himself waiting tables at a local restaurant. On one of his days off, he received a phone call from his ex-boss, Darlene, at the university.

"Tony, I am so glad you picked up the phone!," said Darlene. "I just got wind of an amazing opportunity that you'd be perfect for. What are you doing right now?"

Darlene said the university was looking for a recruiter to travel the state and get high school juniors and seniors to commit and enroll to the university. Darlene had watched Tony develop through the Excellence program and she wanted him to put in for the recruiter position. She believed his excitement for learning, paired with his great presence and speaking skills, would make him a great fit for the job. Darlene also hoped this would push Tony to keep getting better at what he was already showing promise with.

Tony was looking to pursue a career that was more in line with his degree, and he felt this was the perfect opportunity for him. He asked for the contact information of the supervisor and reached out the next day. Within two months, Tony had been offered and accepted the recruiting position. With the new job came a move to the big city and a bunch of new challenges. Despite his initial lack of familiarity with the job's intricacies, he recognized the necessity of paying keen attention during the upcoming training sessions. While memories of the New Start retreat from years ago had mostly faded, some of those invaluable lessons were about to resurface, transforming into powerful guiding messages for Tony.

Armed with just his notepad, an open mind, and a welcoming smile, Tony delved into the training for his new job. The initial hours were dedicated to the fundamentals—policies, procedures, and the responsibilities tied to his position. Following lunch at the university facility, the next speaker took the floor, a professor from the college of Psychology within the same school. Introducing herself as a subject matter expert in social influence, she immediately piqued Tony's interest.

As the professor delved into the intricacies of social influence, Tony's undergraduate studies came rushing back to him. He vividly recalled the fascination he felt exploring how specific behaviors could trigger certain responses in people. Even the seemingly trivial details, like the placement of eyes on a cereal box, could drive kids to entice their parents into purchasing the sweetest breakfast treats. Throughout the presentation, the professor skillfully illustrated how leveraging social influence could empower recruiters to cultivate relationships, establish rapport, and ultimately wield influence with potential applicants and their families. Tony gleaned several crucial insights from the session, including:

- Building likability hinges on genuinely liking others first and demonstrating it.

- Gaining compliance often starts with small gestures, following the rule of reciprocity.

- Securing a commitment from individuals can motivate them to uphold their word consistently.

- Selling ideas can be achieved by referencing what other groups are doing.

- The fear of loss is a potent motivator, as people strive to avoid missing out on opportunities.

- Information presented by or perceived from authority figures increases receptiveness.

- Establishing a sense of unity, emphasizing a collective "we are in this together," fosters influence with others.

Tony took these words to heart and immediately started utilizing them in his office to test their effectiveness with his new co-workers. He would take his notes everywhere with him; he even made another copy just to leave on his desk. Tony actively sought positive qualities in his new colleagues, and before he knew it, he found himself being invited to lunch by his co-workers. Without any expectation of reciprocation, he started bringing coffee to his office mate in the mornings. To his surprise, she responded by bringing him a donut and leaving a thoughtful good morning note.

Notably, this same co-worker jumped to volunteer when Tony needed someone to cover for an event that was in conflict with an important meeting he had scheduled. During a conversation about facing a challenging situation together, as they were both unexpectedly pushed into late overtime, their camaraderie deepened, forging a closer bond in the subsequent days.

As each of these tactics proved successful, Tony couldn't help but think, This stuff really works! Witnessing the effectiveness behind the curtain of influence, he realized there was no turning back.

With his new job, Tony was doing a lot of traveling. He would go from one college fair to another, all over the state, giving presentations about the university to young minds everywhere. Tony thought there couldn't be anything better; he thrived off the nervousness he felt going into every presentation. He was hooked. One night at a college and job fair, Tony met Larry who was set up at the information booth beside him.

Larry, a handsome 30-year old Filipino man with a million-dollar smile, was wearing a prominent badge, crisp blue uniform, and shiny boots. Tony learned that Larry was recruiting for the local police department. As the event unfolded with its cycles of activity and quiet moments, Larry, known for his friendliness, engaged in casual conversation with Tony. It became evident that Larry was employing social influence tactics. A skilled recruiter, Larry complimented Tony multiple times during their interaction and subtly probed if Tony harbored any interest in pursuing a career as a police officer. Tony chuckled at the idea and graciously thanked Larry for his kind words.

As the day wound down, Larry gave Tony a big smile, a firm handshake and his business card, as he said, "We could really use someone great like you."

A few months later, Tony walked into another college fair. These had become old hat for Tony as he was doing more and more presentations. When he took the stage to speak that day, Tony caught Larry's smile in the back of the hall. As always, Larry was beaming with energy, surrounded by people who were eager to talk to him.

After finishing his presentation, Tony made his way to Larry's table. Larry was always popular, so there was a short wait, but as soon as Larry could give his attention he smiled big and shook Tony's hand. As he waited, he'd noticed how Larry always gave people his full attention, as if they were the only people in the room. Larry's approach to communication was noteworthy—he employed kind eyes, a warm smile, and positioned his body entirely towards the person. His friendly demeanor resonated in the tone of his voice. Larry had a knack for asking numerous questions without making it feel rushed, and he listened attentively to each response. Tony observed these effective communication techniques and was eager to learn from Larry's skill in connecting with people. As Larry spoke, Tony felt the impact of these communication strategies, and before he realized it, he found himself filling out an interest card.

It took seven months to undergo the complete application process. A background detective reached out to Tony about two months after he had submitted the interest card and the painstaking process had begun. During this time, Larry was still in touch, which proved to Tony that Larry used his skills to make *real* connections with people. He was genuinely interested in the success of those he was recruiting into the police tribe. Tony made a mental note of this: when you help people, and follow through after helping them, it shows you aren't there to manipulate them.

When Larry had time, he invited Tony to lunch near the police headquarters. As they sat down for some burgers, they joked about the testing process and some of the hoops Tony would have to jump through. Fortunately, Tony had a valuable ally in his background detective, Trudy, who happened to be friends with Larry. Down the road, Tony would learn that Trudy and Larry were long time friends, and they worked well together. Trudy was as welcoming as Larry and had been very attentive to answer any questions throughout the process, calling Tony back quickly whenever he had to leave a message. In turn, Tony felt a sense of reciprocation to Trudy, any time she asked for any additional documentation for reference. Tony didn't want to let her down.

That day, Larry and Tony had a great meal and, as they were sitting, doing some people watching, Larry asked, "Tony, what is it that you want out of this job?"

Violating his normal pattern of communication, Larry immediately added, "And don't give me that canned answer that you want to help people. Returning to his usual speaking style, Larry embraced a moment of silence, his warm smile persisting. This pause prompted Tony to contemplate the question more profoundly, with Larry allowing him the time to formulate a genuine response.

Why did Tony want to do this? He was literally changing his whole career path to do this.

"Well, I do want to help people..." Tony started.

Larry chuckled. "I said no canned answers!"

They both laughed before Tony continued.

"Hear me out, hear me out. I want to learn to be more like you; to talk like you, to treat people like you do. I feel like you're the type of officer I want to be, and it seems like the way you carry yourself would make people more likely to talk to you out there."

Larry, always quick with a smile and a joke, replied, "You know I am not the one who actually hires you, right?"

Tony smiled and felt his face flush. "I mean it, man. And I know this sounds goofy... but would you be willing to mentor me?"

Larry, who hadn't stopped smiling, scooted his chair closer to the table. "Absolutely."

CHAPTER 3

EMBRACE THE SUCK

The first morning of the police academy was a day Tony would always remember. It was a sweltering 98 degrees at 0600, without a hint of a breeze in the desert. Sweat dripped from his brow, and the brows of 45 other cadets who all looked like nervous little penguins in their white long sleeve shirts, black ties, and black slacks. Tony attempted to shine his boots the night before, but lacking any military background or familial ties to the armed forces, his boots were far from the mirrored toe tips sported by some of the recruits.

As he and his classmates cooked under the July sun, a group of four officers donning 'Smokey the Bear' style hats, pressed uniforms, and shiny boots marched with intention towards them. As the class quaked in unison, Tony started to sweat more.

Then the silence broke.

"CLASS 405, ATTENHUT!"

As they had been shown to do, the class snapped to attention. They were then commanded to count off by fives to break into squads. As they went down the line, the stress was too much and one recruit miscounted.

"WHAT THE HELL IS WRONG WITH YOU, RECRUIT!?" yelled one of the training officers.

"Sir, sorry, sir, I have no excuse," replied the recruit.

"YOU ARE SORRY? AREN'T YOU?"

"LET'S TRY THIS AGAIN!" yelled the training officer.

As they came to the recruit who miscounted the first time, his voice broke, but he got the count correct. The count progressed smoothly until it reached the recruit beside Tony, who unfortunately miscounted.

The recruit training officer jumped on it, "HOLY SHIT! WE GOT US A CLASS FULL OF SPECIALS RIGHT HERE, DON'T WE?"

Then came the next command, "FRONT LEANING REST POSITION!"

"THE PUSHUP!" the recruits yelled back in unison. At that moment all the little penguins dropped into the up position of a pushup. And they held and they held and they held.

Another of the recruit training officers started in, "LISTENING TO DIRECTIONS, AND FOLLOWING THEM WILL BE KEY TO YOUR SUCCESS HERE! DO YOU UNDERSTAND?"

The penguins replied, "SIR, YES SIR!" And then they held and held and held as drops of sweat rolled into their eyes.

As the sun ascended directly over the mountain, its rays seemed laser-focused on the black pants Tony wore, and he suddenly realized, I am drenched. The fatigue was evident as the arms of many recruits began to tremble.

The command came, "RECOVER!"

And they did. As the recruits started the count over, Tony realized he was overloaded too. As it came to the person next to him, he kept thinking he was going to screw it up, but somehow he didn't. But three people down, well, that recruit wasn't as lucky.

This resulted in another drop to the "FRONT LEANING REST POSITION" and some more yelling. This time they stayed in the position longer, and Tony could feel that even the rubberized track they were on was starting to get very warm under his hands.

After this berating, they recovered to their standing positions, and just as they were coming to the end of the lecture one of the recruit training officers noticed something. It seemed like it would be inconsequential, but in this context it was a big deal.

The female RTO yelled, "SO, WE HAVEN'T PUT IN ANY OF THE WORK, YET WE SEEM TO BELIEVE THAT ON THE FIRST DAY OF TRAINING WE ARE GOING TO ASSUME WE MADE IT?!"

Another recruit training officer approached her position and inspected what she was indicating. A recruit had brought a gym bag on the first day adorned with the emblem of the police department, featuring his name and the title of "officer" embroidered on it.

One of the male RTO's contorted his face into what looked like a rabid pitbull and quietly said, "Everyone drop their shit."

The penguins dropped everything, and the RTO yelled, "FALL INTO LINE AND FOLLOW ME!"

The next 20 minutes included a nice jogging tour of the academy grounds and surrounding desert, all the while the little penguins, in their little dress clothes, being berated for showing how inept they were. The cadets were assured that the RTO's (great guys and gal that they were!) would work this issue of bravado out of them. When they returned to their spot on the track, not one person in that class had a dry shirt, or pants, and they all fell back to attention. The penguins were then instructed to grab their belongings and were shown to their classroom.

The day continued in the same stressful pattern, with giant binders thrown around the room, a recruit who was supposedly late being fired on the spot (the class would learn after graduation that this was fake), and lots of "FRONT LEANING REST POSITION!" And yelling—*so much yelling.*

Tony, entirely unaccustomed to such an experience, felt profoundly out of his depth. During one of the breaks in the classroom, a robust red-headed individual with closely cropped hair, appearing to be about ten years older than Tony, approached him.

With a deep booming voice he said, "You good?"

Tony took a second to look up. "Yeah man, I'm okay," he replied in a voice Tony didn't even recognize as himself.

"I am Jamie, man. I came out here from Minnesota. It is fucking *hot* out here," he said as he stood there, his face bright red.

Tony was in his own head so deep, he didn't know exactly what he had gotten himself into here, but he wasn't feeling really great, or talkative at that moment. Tony hadn't noticed that a bit of time had lapsed since Jamie last said something.

Jamie filled the silence. "Good talk, buddy," he boomed as he chuckled and started to walk away.

Tony finally replied, "I am sorry man. This is just *a lot.*"

Jamie, in a deep gruff voice that Tony would learn to love over the years, shared, "Hey, I was in the Army as an MP and these are all just games brother. They are pushing us, testing us, and making sure we can listen to direction and perform under stress. It's just that, brother."

Jamie patted Tony on the back solidly, and said, "We got this man, we are in it together."

All of a sudden Tony felt a little better, like he could breathe again.

Not until the weekend, after those first five hellish days, did Tony think about what a good guy Jamie was and how he was creating a unity that not only made Tony feel better in a highly stressful situation, but was also making him feel part of something more. He, along with others, would later call this the 'embrace the suck' effect. Later in his career, Tony would articulate that in situations involving arduous, stressful, or challenging tasks, maintaining unity significantly enhances productivity. In other words, 'This is gonna' fucking suck, but we are in this together, so let's take care of each other and knock this shit out.' If you can make people feel like you are in this together, the tough times seem a little more manageable.

As the weeks flew by, Jamie took Tony under his wing like a little brother. The genuine manner in how he approached Tony that first day didn't change. Jamie never asked for anything in return, but he was there for Tony and willing to listen to him when things got tough. Jamie taught Tony how to shine his boots, how to do better on the parade deck during formation, and even how to keep his pants lint-free. Jamie also helped Tony work through the stress of this new environment and kept him positive when things looked most dreary. It was no easy task when your squadmate gets all their locker contents thrown on the lawn next to the parade deck, and you are down the 'FRONT

LEANING REST POSITION' for a really long time because of that one person not locking their locker fully.

Tony found himself in a world he didn't quite grasp, and the emotions he experienced echoed the overwhelming sensations he felt when playing baseball as a kid. This familiar sense of being completely inundated made Tony harbor a dislike for baseball practice, playing, and any discussions related to the sport. Despite his aversion, his dad insisted on making him attend. Tony hated this same persistent feeling of stress and anxiety but knew this was part of the process Jamie had explained to him.

"You are going into a career that is nothing but stress after stress after stress, brother. They have to know you can handle it long-term or else they are doing you, your fellow officers, and the community a disservice," Jamie had said.

Tony had actually found the academics and physical fitness aspects of the academy to come with ease because of his preparation and schooling, but the scenario, defensive tactics, and firearms training were another story. Jamie remained a steadfast companion for Tony, consistently communicating with a calm and direct tone that reassured Tony that everything would be okay. Tony observed how Jamie's approach to people in various situations had a remarkable calming effect. Ironically, Jamie's skill in handling situations ultimately played a crucial role in saving Tony's life one night.

One Saturday night as Jamie, Tony, and their squadmate Vinnie unwound over beers at a country western bar outside of town, Jamie told Tony, "You have to find a way to push through, man. You are smart, and I could see you climbing up the ladder in this department. Don't let these trainers get you down. When you are Chief, I would like to work for you some day."

They both laughed at that and each took a big swig of whatever cheap draft beer they had ordered. Jamie then slapped Tony on the back and said, "And don't drink too much tonight! I want to get home at a decent time and not have to pull your ass out of any fires tonight, knucklehead!"

As if Tony hadn't listened to anything Jamie said, he had one drink too many that night. A couple of hours into the evening, as he was carrying a pitcher of the same cheap beer back to their table, Tony clumsily bumped into a biker wearing a full patched leather vest at the bar. Tony was too stuporous to think quickly and apologize, so the biker's anger was free to run rampant. Tony, not being in his best state of mind, smarted off to the 'gentleman' and the next thing he knew, the biker was flashing knives at him that he had hidden on the inside of his vest. Luckily, Jamie had only had two beers up until that point and had his wits about him.

Coming around the pool table with a smile, Jamie extended his hand out and, in his deep voice, calmly said, "Hey man, I'm Jamie. You'll have to excuse my friend here, he is an idiot."

Tony looked at Jamie in shock, while Jamie gave Tony his best dad face, communicating, "Shut the hell up!"

The biker yelled, "I ought to take this piece of shit out back and show him what a real man can do to some punk fucking kid!". Jamie's calm demeanor, head nodding and genuine intent didn't change at all during the tirade; he just listened to the biker's rant. This tactic seemed to come through for Tony, and Jamie was able to bring the biker out of his drunk rage after just listening and apologizing to him again. Jamie was so good at what he did that he and the biker shared a beer before Jamie escorted Tony out of the bar for the night. As they caught a ride home, Tony sat in the back seat, dozing off, reflecting on how impressive it was that Jamie could communicate with people so effectively, even in stressful conditions. In that moment, he knew that, somehow, he aspired to be as cool and calm as Jamie someday.

For the rest of the academy, Tony kept a low profile on the weekends and Jamie helped to keep him positive. Tony was ecstatic when he finally made it through to the end. Tony had admitted to himself several times towards the final phases of the academy that he didn't know if he was going to make it because of his anxiety, but he pulled through.

The day of the swearing in ceremony was one he thought he might not see with his class. As he walked on stage to be sworn in, Tony knew that Jamie saved him in more ways than one, and he would not ever forget that. To add to the awesome feeling of accomplishment, Larry had shown up to the event looking sharp as ever and smiling that million-watt smile Tony spotted as soon as he walked in the auditorium. When it came time for the pinning of badges, Tony asked Larry if would do the honors. Larry, beaming with happiness, was more than willing to place Tony's badge on him, before giving him a big bear hug.

"Thank you for the honor, my friend," he said.

As the ceremony wound down, the new rookies dispersed throughout the auditorium, meeting with their loved ones to discuss plans for post-ceremony celebrations. Tony found himself engaged in conversation with some family friends, his uncle, little cousin, mom, and dad when Larry approached from behind, embracing him in another hug. Laughter ensued as Tony introduced Larry to his family. Despite hearing Tony mention Larry and Jamie over the past year, Tony's family, not fully supportive of his decision to become an officer, hadn't paid much attention to the stories he had shared. Tony briefly excused himself from the group to have a private conversation with Larry.

Larry looked at him intensely with a smile and said, "Brother, you are *the* man!"

Tony smiled, and thanked Larry, remembering all the great advice and support he'd received from him. Tony briefly wondered if Larry would still be as proud of him, knowing the stress he had been under for the past four months, but he swiftly pushed that thought aside.

Larry continued, "I have got you all set up, man. Nick, who you know, is going to train you out on the Westside, bro!"

Tony knew Nick from some night classes he'd been taking before the academy. He knew him to be a friendly, sharp, educated, and physical guy. Tony was humbled and excited that he would get to train under Nick. This news just put a cherry on top of the day.

As Tony and his family walked out of the hall to head to dinner, he looked over at Jamie and mouthed, "THANK YOU!"

Jamie just grinned and said, "See ya' next week, knucklehead."

The following two weeks, known as post-academy, were much lighter. They were now officers on the academy grounds, so there was no more saluting the staff and no more required tests or scenarios. The new officers were now learning details about what was expected of them during field training, like how to use a taser, extra defensive tactics, and very specific agency policy training. As the two weeks came to an end, everyone was a little nervous again knowing assignments would soon be handed out.

Tony for once felt confident because he knew that Larry and Nick were making sure he was going to be successful. As the Friday before field training started, the field training officers (FTOs) milled around the room where they had been reporting for post academy every morning. Tony didn't see anyone he recognized amongst the FTO's and he wondered where Nick was.

CHAPTER 4

A BOY NAMED SUE

Seated, Tony felt a slight confusion creeping in. There was a subtle feeling that things were regressing, as the new officers in the room appeared tense, staring forward at the front of the room, sitting upright—reminiscent of their posture during the early days of the academy over four months ago. The academy Sergeant stepped forward and began reading off Field Training Officer assignments. Tony attempted to steal another glance around the back of the room but failed to spot Nick's athletic, 6'4" frame anywhere in the room.

Finally, the Sergeant read Tony's name and followed with, "Leslie Fachnan."

Tony's mind started to race. Who was Leslie? he wondered.

As the last names were read off the list, the room came alive again.

Jamie looked over at Tony, "You good?"

Tony nodded, but he was not good. He was confused.

Then Tony heard a gruff voice he hadn't expected. "Hey, I am Leslie. Let's go talk."

Tony stood up quickly as to not be disrespectful, and introduced himself to Leslie with a firm handshake and respectful eye contact. He then followed Leslie out of the room, into the parade deck area. Leslie looked to be about 40 and stood at about 5'9". He had a thinnish build and was kind of average-looking, with a red face, squinty eyes, and a very pronounced flattop. His uniform was clean and pressed, and he carried himself with a sort of swagger that didn't quite fit him, like an extra in an episode of "Gunsmoke."

As they stepped away from the others, Leslie started in a voice that was a significant pitch higher than when he had initially introduced himself. "So, listen, I have heard all about you. Nick thinks you're a good guy and I am sure he is right, but Nick is actually in a new detail now, so I ended up stuck with you." This was not a promising introduction for Tony. Leslie looked Tony straight in the eye with such strong intensity before continuing.

"Look, I am sure you are some kind of whiz kid with your college degree, but I could give two shits. I am sick and tired of people coming into my department thinking they know everything, so you better not be one of those or you won't last."

Tony, trying his best to suppress his shock, replied, "No sir."

Leslie smirked and responded, "Good then, we should get along fine."

Tony was still in shock that this was happening. He had been so ready to be trained by someone he knew was easy-going but this was going to be much different. Leslie continued on his spiel, telling Tony what he expected the first day of the next week. "You better be ready to fucking work."

Tony was respectful the whole time and when the conversation finished he said, "Thank you, sir. I'm looking forward to it." The interaction had taken all of ten minutes, but Tony could tell this was going to be a different kind of challenge.

Tony tried not to stress about the first day too much over the next weekend. At the time, Tony was dating a really nice girl who had seen the stress in him over the last five months and was always trying to lighten his load. She had taken him that weekend to camp in the woods, celebrate the academy graduation and relax a bit. While Tony appreciated the sweet gesture and did relax quite a bit that weekend, he couldn't help but have a looming feeling that something bad was coming Monday. Tony showed up on Monday for the swing shift, his shirt and pants pressed, his badge and shoes shined, and with all his required equipment ready to go.

The precinct was an older building that had a moist and musty, almost basement-like, smell to it. The exterior paint appeared dull and weathered, while the interior suffered from peeling. The lighting in the halls emitted a harsh, white fluorescent glow that prompted squints from anyone who entered. As he stepped into the briefing room, Tony saw the distressed look on the faces of his fellow squadmates who had ended up in the same precinct; Jamie wasn't one of them. Seated at the front of the room, everyone gazed intently at the whiteboard, their field training binders laid out before them, and a noticeable silence prevailed.

In contrast, the Field Training Officers occupied the back of the room—some engaged in light banter, others chatting on the phone, and a few discreetly spitting chewing tobacco into empty water bottles. Leslie was not in the room when Tony walked in. He took his seat with his classmates, some forcing smiles towards him. They were all a bit on edge. Shortly after, Leslie walked into the briefing room while talking on his cell phone. Leslie's face was bright red, and he sounded upset as he hung up the phone.

He had a clear look of frustration about him. Tony didn't even want to make eye contact, so he just looked straight ahead.

The squad Sergeant walked into the briefing room right on time and quietly closed the door. She had a kind look and introduced herself as Terri as she turned off the television that had been on in the background. Right off the bat, Terri seemed very approachable and warm. She told the group that if they needed anything, they could feel free to speak with her, as it was her job to help them succeed.

Tony was struck by the confidence of the Sergeant, who held a higher rank than everyone in the room, yet encouraged people to address her by her first name. He found this intriguing, and it also caught his attention that, despite the invitation, everyone still referred to her as 'Sarge' out of respect.

The Sergeant welcomed the new officers in training and then went over some issues going on in the precinct. She spoke about some trends that had come up with paperwork and a string of car burglaries occurring at multiple apartment complexes in the precinct.

As Sergeant Terri finished up the briefing, she told everyone to "Be safe, and do good work out there."

Tony then heard Leslie. "Hey rook, here are the keys. Get your shit loaded up, get her gassed up, and then meet me at my truck."

Tony took the keys from Leslie, walked out and did as he was told. He made sure to keep his uniform as clean as possible as he was gassing up the car and checking tire pressures. As he made his way back, he just couldn't shake the nervousness. He thanked God that it wasn't summer in the desert to add intense sweating to his anxiety. Tony pulled the Crown Victoria to Leslie's pickup, and Leslie put a bag in the trunk.

"I'll be driving today," Leslie informed Tony.

A small sense of relief washed over Tony, alleviating some of the stress associated with navigating the unfamiliar neighborhood for calls. As they pulled out of the precinct lot, Leslie gave another spiel about what he expected from Tony, which Tony had expected. But this time, Leslie kept referring to the precinct as "*my* precinct" which struck Tony as a bit odd. As they took their first call, Leslie said he would handle it and Tony could just watch. Following instructions, Tony paid close attention to how the simple burglary call was handled. After they left the scene, Leslie broke down the call in a manner that was quite understandable. Then, Leslie took a phone call.

As soon as he got off the phone, Leslie said, "Alright, we are headed to go help your buddy out."

Tony looked at Leslie quizzically.

"Your buddy Nick and his guys are after this kid with a felony warrant," Leslie explained. "Let's see if those legs of yours are as fast as Nick says."

Tony hadn't remembered telling Nick anything about his running ability, and he definitely was *not* the fastest person in his academy class. He didn't know why Leslie would say that, but it was apparently 'go time.'

As they drove into the neighborhood, Tony was trying to pay attention to where they were, but he didn't recognize any of the street names. Next thing he knew he saw a Hispanic male with a shaved head in a dark hoodie and jeans run past their car into some yards.

Leslie yelled out, "Get out and get him!"

Tony didn't know what the hell was going on, but with a direct order from his field training officer, he jumped out of the car as it slowed to a stop.

Tony took off after the suspect and, for the first time, realized, "Crap, this is a lot different than a sprint." As he ran, Tony felt his vest pressing against his chest, impeding his ability to move and breathe. His gun belt shifted with the lopsided weight of his pistol on one side, and his radio smacked his back with each stride. The boots he wore were far from optimal for chasing people. The uneven weight distribution of the gun belt was impacting the direction of Tony's movement more than he had initially thought. Setting those thoughts aside, he adjusted his gait and pushed himself to run as hard as he could. A small smile formed on his face as he closed in on the suspect. Tony was just a few steps behind when the subject dashed into a driveway and hopped onto the hood of a white SUV.

Tony thought to himself, *Now I've got him.*

As Tony leaped to grab the suspect's hoodie on the car, he quickly realized that his expectations didn't align with reality; the movement in uniform was different from being out of uniform. The added weight prevented him from reaching as far as he thought he could without the equipment, and his gun belt got snagged on the side of the car, momentarily stopping him. Tony recovered swiftly, but before he could make another move, a uniformed officer appeared out of nowhere and tackled the suspect. Tony was a close second to the subject, who fought vigorously to escape. Suddenly, a massive body joined the pile, halting the suspect's attempts to break free. It was Nick, who flashed a big smile as he held the suspect's shoulders down. They successfully took the suspect into custody, and just as quickly as it had started, the chase came to an end.

Tony stood the suspect up and they walked him to the closest patrol vehicle.

Nick walked up behind Tony and put his giant hand on his shoulder, "Great job, brother!"

"I lost him," said Tony, dejected.

"Oh man, I lose more people than I catch. That's why we're a team." Nick's kindness was welcome, but it still stung that he hadn't caught his first chase on his own, especially to help Nick.

Nick then said, "And I am sorry things didn't work out how we had thought man, this gig is a good opportunity I couldn't pass up."

Tony told Nick he completely understood and thanked him for all his help along the way.

"I gotta get this dude booked, but we need to do lunch," said Nick as he parted ways.

Tony said a quick goodbye with a handshake and turned around. Leslie sauntered up with a smirk on his face.

"Well, dust yourself off," Leslie said, turning to walk back to the car. Tony cleaned himself up the best he could and made his way to the car.

As he sat in the passenger seat Leslie said, "Well, you really fucked that one up, huh, college boy?"

Looking back now, Tony wished he had shown enough confidence to stop Leslie right then and there. But, at that time, Tony was just 24; a young man in a world that he didn't quite understand. So he sat quietly, staring out the passenger window as his face flushed with embarrassment. Tony finished out the shift with some simple trespassing calls and a vehicle theft, but he left that day feeling pretty worthless.

To top it all off, Leslie approached Tony as he was completing some reports and informed him that the neighbor, whose car Tony had unintentionally collided with during the chase, had filed a complaint about the damage to her vehicle. Further compounding the situation, Leslie handed Tony the three reports he had submitted, each covered in red ink for corrections.

"Don't know about this college education, seems like you write like crap to me," Leslie chided.

He then walked out of the room. Tony didn't finish with the corrections until two hours after his shift had already ended; he was exhausted. As he drove home, he couldn't help but feel like his first day was pretty damn rough. Tony's confidence was low, and he wasn't looking forward to tomorrow.

CHAPTER 5

THE DECISION

It was the start of the eighth week of field training and Tony hadn't been doing well. It seemed as though every decision he made was the wrong one and that every report he turned in was garbage. He had been getting held over every night for report issues, and he didn't understand how his writing could be so off given how many papers he had written over the years. He knew he wasn't an amazing author, but never before had he felt this inept.

Adding to the challenges, stress began to interfere with Tony's sense of direction when responding to calls, prompting Leslie to start reprimanding him on the way to assignments. This consistent stress persisted throughout the entire training day, creating an unending cycle of feeling like a failure every day, compounded by being told how much of a failure he was. Despite reaching out to Jamie, who assured him everything would be fine, Tony couldn't shake the overwhelming feeling of unease.

As Tony gassed up and headed over to Leslie's truck like normal, he could see Leslie on the phone. He was once again red-faced and looked like he might be arguing with someone. The driver's side window was down so he could hear Leslie cursing. Tony just knew he was in for it that day. He had parked and waited for about five minutes as Leslie finished his argument. He then threw his gear in the trunk and slammed it. Leslie got in the passenger seat and didn't say much.

They were soon responding to a wreck and Tony handled the call without issue. Their next call was a domestic violence incident, which came in with a sense of urgency due to it being a violent crime in progress. A neighbor had reported what they believed to be an ongoing assault between a boyfriend and girlfriend residing in the house next to the 911 caller. Upon parking two houses down from the provided address, Tony observed the male involved in the incident running from the front yard into the home's carport.

Leslie hustled over to the carport and Tony followed. Tony wondered why they were in such a rush to chase this guy into an unknown area, but he wasn't in charge. The male, who had tucked himself behind an old car, started yelling obscenities and refused to come out of the driveway. The suspect sounded drunk as he slurred his speech.

The woman from the home managed to come out through the front door, displaying visible bruising that clearly resulted from the altercation. Another officer who arrived promptly after Leslie and Tony began interviewing her. Meanwhile, Leslie found himself in a heated confrontation with the suspect, with neither side willing to back down. Sensing an opportunity, Tony stepped in to address the suspect. Drawing on a memory from months ago when Jamie had helped diffuse a situation in a bar, Tony offered the guy a kind smile.

Tony then calmly said, "Hey brother, my name is Tony."

The man replied, "I'll talk to you but fuck that other guy!"

Leslie started to cuss back at the man, but Tony interrupted Leslie. "It's okay, you and I can talk."

The dialogue continued from there. Tony utilized patience and, while he didn't always know exactly what to say, he figured if he kept the guy talking, at least he wasn't attacking them.

Tony asked, "Are you OK?"

Leslie turned to Tony and shot him a disapproving look. "What the fuck are you doing?" Leslie asked.

Tony looked at Leslie and whispered, "Let me try this."

Leslie's face turned redder than usual.

Tony continued to talk to the husband, asking him again, "Sir, are you OK?"

"My wife attacked me with a kitchen knife!" the man yelled in distress, before raising his forearm to show some defensive wounds, covered in blood.

"OK," Tony replied. "We can get the fire department here to take a look at those cuts for you."

The husband muttered, "Thanks, but no thanks."

"So, how did this all start?" Tony continued.

At this point, more officers were arriving at the scene and the Sergeant from an adjacent beat area had arrived. Leslie had stormed off and was now speaking with the Sergeant. As Tony continued talking with the man, he learned that he and his wife had been fighting for some time and they were under a lot of pressure at the moment because they'd been evicted from their home. Tony was doing his best to follow the husband's story as he slurred it out, but he learned that the wife had attacked her husband because he had been 'too friendly' with the cashier at the local liquor store earlier that evening. As the husband's story continued, his demeanor subsequently calmed.

Without warning, two officers came up from the left of where Tony was standing behind another vehicle in the driveway, and he heard a series of loud "bam" noises.

The next moment caught Tony off guard as officers rushed in and apprehended the husband, who was now on the ground in evident pain. Tony was in shock, primarily because no one had informed him about the unfolding plan and also because he was in the midst of speaking with the husband when things took this unexpected turn. The officers who had positioned themselves beside Tony had utilized a stun-bag shotgun to incapacitate the husband. Tony, feeling that the situation had considerably calmed down and was moving in a positive direction, couldn't comprehend the sudden shift.

As he walked back towards the car, Leslie yelled, "Rook, get over here and search this guy before you put him in our car!"

Tony walked over to the husband who was being stood up by the other officers. The husband turned to him and said, "Fuck you, man! You lied to me, acting like you were trying to help me."

Tony stayed quiet, feeling bad about being accused of such deceitfulness. He escorted the man to their Crown Victoria, searched him and placed him in the back. The man looked Tony dead in the eyes with an icy cold glare as he sat him down.

"Don't do that shit to people, man. I would have come out to you. I knew I was going to jail, bro. Acting like you're going to help me and then tricking me before you hurt them is just *wrong*."

Tony gave the man an apologetic look. He closed the door and finished the investigation. It was a difficult one because the woman had fresh bruising and marks on her arms, which she received prior to defending herself with a kitchen knife. The fire department came and checked on both the wife and the husband, patching up and bandaging his cut wounds. Tony and Leslie then transported the male to the precinct for booking.

As Tony drove, Leslie stared out the window and said, "Well, you screwed that one up huh, college boy?"

As they pulled into the precinct, Tony escorted the man into the booking area and started his paperwork for processing. Leslie disappeared into the precinct as usual. Tony worked quietly as the husband sat cuffed to a nearby bench.

The man then said, "I know you didn't mean to screw me over, bro."

Tony looked at his computer screen. "Thanks," he said. "I really was trying to help you."

"Those other guys were just there to hurt me, man. I could tell by the way you were talking to me that you really were trying to keep me safe. I saw how you acted after they shot me with that crap, they didn't tell you what they were going to do."

"I appreciate it, sir," said Tony. "I honestly was hoping to talk with you until we could come to an understanding, and I am sorry your night ended like this." Tony finished the paperwork and then requested for a wagon over the radio to take the man to central booking.

As Tony sat in the back office working on the report for the domestic violence call, he couldn't help but wonder what he could have done better to help resolve the situation. From his psych classes in school, he knew he could have communicated better, but under the stress he couldn't remember any of the tricks he had picked up along the way.

He then overheard Leslie in the hall talking about the call, and as he was explaining it, Leslie said, "We just didn't have time to be dicking around with this guy who is threatening us. So, I told Sarge we had a threat situation that needed to be met with force."

Tony had not seen the situation this way, but who was he to confront his training officer? Tony finished the report and turned it over to Leslie. Leslie made a few red marks on it and handed it back.

Before Tony could turn around Leslie started, "Listen Antonio, I don't think you are cut out for this...."

Tony felt a tightness settle into his chest, and his jaw set. "Here we are tonight, dealing with some asshole criminal, and you're over there trying to have a conversation with him," added Leslie.

Tony choked out an, "I am sorry."

Before stepping out of the room, Leslie said, "I just really think you should consider doing something else college boy, this ain't it for ya."

Tony finished corrections on the report and submitted it. He then changed in the locker room and kept himself from tearing up as he dressed down into his street clothes. Tony hadn't felt this alone ever, and it was a heavy weight. He drove home and went straight to sleep.

The next morning, Tony woke up and was still weighed down from the sadness of the eight previous weeks, but even moreso from the interaction the night before. As he sat sipping some instant coffee with creamer, watching the morning news, he wondered what would happen if he decided to quit.

All of a sudden, he felt a rush of relief, like a wave had just lifted the weight he hadn't even realized he was carrying off his chest. Tony didn't want to throw away all the hard work he had done, but he also didn't want to keep feeling like an idiot day in and day out. As he sat there alone and pondered, he knew the answer. Tony showered, brushed his teeth, and threw some gel in his hair. He was ready. As Tony drove to the precinct a few minutes early, he felt lighter than he had in a long while. As he pulled into the gated lot, he knew exactly what he was going to say. Tony walked in to find Sergeant Terri in her office.

She smiled. "Antonio, good to see you. What can I do for you?"

Tony sat down with a heavy half-smile. "Sarge, I appreciate everything you have done for me, but I am done." The conversation that ensued was one filled with kindness and empathy.

Sergeant Terri asked, "What can I do to help?"

Tony thanked the Sergeant for being so understanding and patient, explaining that he was comfortable with his decision. Sergeant Terri talked about some potential alternatives, but Tony couldn't be swayed. Tony did have a slight sense of guilt, feeling like he was letting Sergeant Terri down. Her tone and probing questions momentarily made him contemplate staying. However, ultimately, Tony adhered to his decision and surrendered his badge, gun, and equipment to the Sarge.

As he walked out, he felt a smile creeping up from deep inside him.

As he got about 50 feet from the building Tony's classmate Nicole ran out of the building calling to him, "Tony, wait!"

Tony turned, and he could see the tears welling up in her eyes.

"Don't bail on me," she said.

"I'm sorry but I just can't do this anymore," Tony replied.

Tony became the second person in their training class to resign, with the first quitting two weeks earlier, and now Nicole would be the last of the three. She looked down sadly, avoiding Tony's gaze, and wished him the best of luck. Turning away, she walked slowly back into the building. Tony made his way to his car and drove out of the precinct gate, feeling a profound sense of relief as he ventured down the street, hoping to leave the precinct as a distant memory.

CHAPTER 6

THE BUG

It was Monday morning, marking one week after Tony had walked away from the precinct. The buzzing cell phone on Tony's nightstand woke him up. Tony, still groggy, reached over, accidentally knocking over a bottle of water before finally grabbing the phone. "Hello?" he answered.

Larry's voice came across the line, "Broooooooooooo, what happened?"

Tony took a deep breath and explained his decision to Larry, answering some questions along the way and giving some backstory about the last two months.

"Leslie just hated me man, and I couldn't seem to get around that. Once he made me feel like an idiot, I just could not shake it. It seemed like everything I did was a mistake", Tony explained.

"Dude, you could have come to me. We could have fixed this," said Larry.

"I am sorry brother, I should have, but I didn't want to be 'that guy' whining and calling in favors."

"I have heard a lot of bad things about Leslie," Larry said, "and I am so sorry you ended up with him. Things should have been different; you are a good guy. Dang it, man!"

Tony felt a rush of shame, embarrassment, and sadness. He apologized again to Larry, and before they hung up the line, they promised each other they would get lunch soon.

Tony had already had a few of these types of conversations over the past week and actually had planned lunch that day with a classmate of his that everyone called Frenchie. Tony showered and threw on a T-shirt, shorts, and tennis shoes before heading out of the house. He met Frenchie and his wife at a small Mexican restaurant. When he walked in Frenchie stood up and gave him a hug, which was not characteristic of him. Tony was surprised that Frenchie had even reached out to him at all after he'd left. Once seated, the conversation was light while they settled in and enjoyed some chips and salsa.

After they ordered their meals and the waitress walked off, Frenchie asked, "So what's the plan now, man?"

Tony shared that his girlfriend at the time worked at her parents' restaurant, and she had offered him a job waiting tables on the weekends. Tony didn't mind that; he had experience waiting tables in college. He liked talking with people and loved being on his feet.

"That's good, man. Glad you have something lined up. But are you sure about this?"

Tony looked at Frenchie, confused. "I already quit, man. What are you talking about?"

"They would take you back," Frenchie explained. "They would be crazy not to, but I know they will, maybe put you with a different trainer, in a different precinct."

"I can't see myself groveling for my job back, bro. And I don't want to come back as 'that guy.' I would never get any respect," said Tony.

Frenchie then started telling Tony about how he left law enforcement four years before their academy class. "I was positive I was done after those first few years and seeing my squadmate shot, but after a while the bug was still there."

Tony questioned, "The bug?"

"Yeah, man. The cop bug. It doesn't just go away. This job is one of the last great adventures. Think about all we can do and see while we are on patrol. All the adrenaline we can take is up for grabs, plus free drinks at Circle K, dude," replied Frenchie with a smile.

"I guess," said Tony.

"Look man, you got a bad roll of the dice for a trainer. That does suck, but just hear me out. And you know what, maybe another department is even a better fit for you, something a little less hectic."

Tony smiled and thanked Frenchie for the advice. They finished their meal and said their goodbyes with a strong handshake.

As they walked out of the restaurant and parted ways Frenchie said, "You're a good guy man, don't give up on this dream."

Some weeks passed and Tony was enjoying the restaurant work. He had also picked up a job as a recruiter for a medical school in the suburb to the east. Tony was super busy, but when he had down time he felt a deep regret about quitting the force, letting his squadmates down, and embarrassing himself. Tony was drinking more than he usually did on his nights off and he just felt worthless.

Frenchie's words kept playing in his head over and over. Yeah, man. The cop bug. It doesn't just go away.

Tony was finding this to be a very true statement as he kept wondering what things would have been like had he only had a different training experience, had he been smarter, had he handled the stress better. This thought kept running through Tony's head until he found himself poking around on his laptop at different smaller agencies. He brushed the idea off initially and thought he might not be thinking clearly as he closed the laptop and went to sleep that night.

Later that week, in the early morning hours, Tony sat up in bed watching a rerun. Feeling the itch for something new, he opened his laptop and started exploring various cities' websites, letting his mind wander into the realm of 'what ifs'. As he browsed, he found himself casually filling out some digital interest cards, thinking it couldn't hurt anything.

Completing three interest cards, he felt a momentary panic after hitting submit. However, he reassured himself, thinking, *There's no way any of these departments would want a washout from training.* He smiled sadly and closed the laptop. As the white light from the screen faded, he sat in the dark, lost in his thoughts until he drifted off to sleep.

The next few days kept Tony busy as he worked hard at the school, attempting to grasp his new job while also waitering on the weekends for some additional income. As the weekend came to a close, he enjoyed a Sunday off. However, by midday, he started feeling extremely lethargic and unmotivated. Initially brushing it off, he attempted to go for a run, hoping to sweat out whatever was affecting him. Ironically, as he jogged that evening, he passed by Frenchie and Dave, both classmates, who were handling a disturbance scene at a McDonald's in his neighborhood. They seemed surprised when he ran by and waved.

Frenchie yelled, "You stalking us now, or what?"

Tony hollered back, "You wish, buddy!" and kept on his path. Tony smiled. When he turned around at the two-mile mark and headed back, Frenchie and Dave were no longer at the McDonald's.

At that moment Tony thought to himself, "Damnit, that should have been me."

The next morning Tony woke up feeling worse. He called in from his work at the school, even though he didn't have any sick days at that point, which really stressed him out. He apologized to his supervisor who was understanding and told Tony to get better. The flu Tony caught would end up taking him down for a whole week. Tony wondered if all the stress and hours of work had just finally caught up to him.

As he was sleeping on the second day of being sick, a phone call startled him and he answered groggily, "Hello."

The voice on the other line had a country twang to it, "Yes, I am looking for Antonio Mendoza."

Tony replied in his raspy voice, "Yessir, you've got him," and then stifled a cough.

"Weeeell, my name is Ron Finkle, I am the Assistant Chief here in Little Green Valley. You put in an interest card with us."

Tony felt a rush of excitement and thought, *Oh my God, these guys want the washout.*

The Assistant Chief continued. "Yes sir, we are looking for some good officers and are more than willing to accept your paperwork if you'd be willing to submit."

Tony thanked the Assistant Chief for his call and let him know he was interested. Tony explained the Readers' Digest version of his situation, without throwing mud on the previous department. The Assistant Chief, in his southern twang, told Tony he would be a welcome addition if he met the department criteria. He then instructed Tony how to apply and thanked him again for his interest. When Tony got off the phone, he felt the endorphins rushing through him from the call.

He felt better for a second before remembering how sick he was and went back to sleep for the rest of the day.

When Tony woke up the next day, he was still sick and a little weak but getting better. Covering himself with eucalyptus oil sent by his mom for his cough, Tony had gone a bit overboard and ended up burning his nose by applying too much oil directly to his face in a desperate attempt for relief. Chuckling at the absurdity of giving himself a chemical burn on and in his nose, he sighed, winced as he washed his face, and lay back down for a bit. Grabbing his laptop, he started working on his application for the Little Green Valley P.D. While at it, he made a mental note to review the background packet he had initially submitted to his previous agency, ensuring that all his answers were consistent with the current application. He didn't want the background detectives to question any of his responses.

As Tony searched for copies of the forms he had filled out previously, he stumbled upon some notes he had prepared for himself in anticipation of his oral board interviews. Larry had shared some tips with him for the oral boards, and the list read:

- Give good, 'kind' eye contact when you are in the room.
- Know the department's mission and frame your answers to it.
- Listen to the questions to understand what they ask, and pause before answering.

- One reversal question can be helpful in showing your skills.
- Sell yourself through vision. Paint them a picture of what you bring to the table.
- Visualize over and over before going into the interview to see yourself succeeding.

Tony had completely forgotten about this preparation from a year ago. He was really happy that he had kept and found these notes. He put them aside on his nightstand and continued looking for the paperwork he needed to fill out.

Tony's experience with the Little Green Valley P.D. proved to be markedly different from his last agency. This time around, the process moved much faster, and before he knew it, he was driving two hours for a ride-along with an officer from the department. Walking into the police department on a Saturday afternoon, Tony was dressed in slacks and a collared shirt, prepared for the swing shift. He rang the bell at the unmanned front desk, and a woman emerged to inquire about his needs.

Tony smiled and introduced himself. "I am an applicant for lateral transfer and here for my ride-along."

The woman welcomed him and asked him to remain in the lobby until his officer was ready for him. Tony thanked the woman, who he would later learn was a dispatcher for the department, and took a seat.

As Tony waited, he reviewed a couple of things from Larry that he wanted to make sure to do. Larry had told him, "Be confident. Don't act like you are desperate for the job, but also show that you feel this could be your place, if you like it."

Larry had also mentioned how important this ride-along would be because this officer's impression of Tony could make or break his application process—especially in a smaller department. Tony had been thinking about this a lot so that he could strike the balance.

Larry had also told him, "You gotta come in and show an interest about the person you're riding with and the department without being annoying."

When Larry told Tony this over the phone the night before, Tony replied, "You lost me."

"It means that you have to ask questions that matter, questions that demand an answer, but not in an annoying way," Larry explained "So, you do that through asking 'what's' and 'how's', stick to asking 'what' and 'how' questions and then shut up and listen."

Larry had also advised Tony to seek permission from the officers to take notes. If granted approval, Tony was encouraged to jot down as much as he could—for his own learning and to convey to the officers that their insights were valuable to him.

Tony waited for about 20 minutes in the lobby and wondered if they had forgotten about him. As he was peeking out the window to the parking lot, the interior lobby door opened up. Out walked a heavier set, 30-year-old officer with a conservative haircut. He introduced himself as Mark and had a goofy smile. Mark waved Tony into the building. He apologized for the wait and explained to Tony that they don't start their shifts at the station.

"We have take-home vehicles, so I start my shift from home. Saves on my 'me' time," Mark said with pride. Mark shared that he used to be a dispatcher and had upgraded to officer about two years ago. Mark was very welcoming as he showed Tony around the newer facility and said that this was a big upgrade from what they used to have. Tony was impressed that a smaller agency had such a nice facility. As Tony walked along, he quickly noticed that Mark was very friendly and liked to talk. Tony thought this would be a perfect opportunity for him to practice what Larry had suggested. As they walked out into the backlot Tony thanked Mark for taking him. Before he could unlock that door to the police Impala, his phone rang.

Mark answered, "Yeah boss, okay we are coming back in."

Tony followed Mark back inside to the Sergeant's office and there sat a giant of a man with a tiny toothpick in his mouth. Tony was honestly taken aback at the man seated with his back to the window. The giant stood up and was just under 7 feet tall and was heavier. As he stood up, he stepped towards Tony, extending his giant hand out.

In a deep, booming, yet surprisingly friendly voice he said, "Hey there, I'm Tom Bartlett." As they shook hands, Tony's hand vanished into the giant grip, and he couldn't help but think, This guy could literally rip my arm off.

"Hello sir, I'm Antonio Mendoza," Tony said, with respectful eye contact and a firm 'tiny' grip.

Sergeant Bartlett responded, "Nice to meet you, Antonio. Please have a seat." Following that, the Sergeant inquired about Tony, who tactfully explained his purpose for being there, emphasizing his eagerness to learn about both the Sergeant and Mark and their department.

He then followed by asking Sergeant Bartlett, "How long have you been here, sir?"

Sergeant Bartlett smiled, shifted in his seat and he started to share his story. He had grown up in Little Green Valley and had been at the department for 23 years. He also shared that he had been a Sergeant for a long time. Tony made sure he was using the skills Larry had suggested to him. He stayed engaged, nodded his head, and followed along with the Sergeant's history.

Tony asked about the department's mission and Sergeant Bartlett smiled even more, discussing the department and his own personal philosophy for policing.

At one point Tony asked Sergeant Bartlett if he could take notes and the Sergeant said, "Yes, of course."

After about an hour of conversation Sergeant Bartlett said, "It has been a pleasure, but I am sure you want to get out there, it has been nice talking with you."

He then said, "Listen, nothing against you, I know you are an officer already, but I don't know you so please stay in the car unless Mark says you're good to come out." Tony acknowledged that he understood and thanked Sergeant Bartlett for his time.

While patrolling the small town with Mark, Tony ensured to ask insightful questions and took detailed notes. Mark, being friendly, shared a lot about the little town. Despite responding to several calls, they were all minor in nature. Mark said it was a slower Saturday than usual, clarifying that they typically dealt with more domestics and fights. Tony would later discover in his career that this phenomenon was known as the 'Curse of the Ride-Along.' Nevertheless, Tony appreciated the slower pace as it provided more opportunities to ask meaningful questions.

The most insightful question of the night that Tony had asked was, "So, Mark, what can I do to be successful here?"

"Man, that's a good question. Honestly, just hustling the radio, shagging calls, and catching drunk drivers."

Tony said, "Okay, so chasing radio calls and D.U.I. investigations."

Mark replied, "Yeah, man."

Mark openly discussed his perspective on the department's culture, revealing details about certain problematic individuals and ongoing issues. Tony diligently documented these insights to gain a better understanding of the department's dynamics. This conversation proved invaluable during Tony's subsequent hiring process and his initial years in the department. To cap off the night, Mark and Tony responded to an incident in the campground at the north end of town. Someone had illicitly entered the camp area and stolen four generators from campers as they slept, consuming the remainder of their shift.

Tony stepped in and helped Mark by taking field interviews of victims and getting information for reports to make Mark's night a little easier. Tony loved this, and he couldn't help but smile at the cool forest air in the middle of May, and the heavy smell of pine in the air.

After responding to the theft call, Mark expressed gratitude to Tony as they headed back to the station and remarked, "I think you'll really like it here, man."

Tony smiled in response and thanked Mark for showing him around and providing answers to his questions.

CHAPTER 7

PUTTING IT ALL ON THE LINE

In June of that year, when the job offer came, Tony eagerly seized the opportunity. His parents facilitated the transition by purchasing Tony's home in the big city as an investment, allowing Tony to make the move to the mountains of Little Green Valley. Jamie, who Tony still stayed in touch with, played a crucial role in assisting Tony with the move, for which Tony was immensely grateful. About halfway during the drive up the mountain Jamie started, "You have to get out of your own head brother. I have watched you struggle with this before and for you to be successful you will need to believe in yourself. You are smart as hell brother, but you have to find a way to put that brain to actual work."

At one point, Jamie took a more serious tone, "You are buying a house here and moving your life. You don't have a choice, you have to succeed." The overarching message was Jamie's belief that this could be a fantastic opportunity for Tony, expressing confidence in his ability to excel in the job. Once they finished unloading Tony's modest belongings, Jamie embraced him warmly and reminded him to be cautious.

"No shenanigans at the bars, I ain't here to save your ass," Jamie joked as he jumped into his pickup and backed out of the driveway.

Seated in a camp chair on his front porch, Tony let out a deep sigh with a whiskey in hand just as a refreshing monsoon rain began. In that moment, he marveled at the journey that brought him to this point. A broad smile stretched across his face as he inhaled deeply, taking in the cool, moist mountain air. Sipping his whiskey, he relished the rhythmic melody of raindrops cascading around him.

As Tony sat on the porch he reflected deeply on his past. While he had done really well on the academic side, he had a difficult time actually applying the laws and concepts of the academy to police street work. Tony was determined to bridge this gap and learn from his field trainer in order to be successful out there.

Tony's trainer in Little Green Valley ended up being a very intense officer named Thomas Hendricks. Thomas was quiet and very well-respected in the small community. A known hard worker, he was athletic, loved to run, was a firearms instructor, and a member of the regional S.W.A.T. team. Upon discovering that he would be training under Thomas, Tony felt a slight intimidation. However, his newfound mindset reassured him that the trainer's identity wouldn't determine his success. Tony swiftly grasped that Thomas was of the quieter disposition, validating Larry's counsel about posing meaningful questions. Recognizing the significance of note-taking, Tony made a mental note to engage in this practice whenever time allowed. Tony had found some of his old college notes in the move and decided he wanted to try to utilize some skills to win over his new trainer and maybe even utilize it on the street. Tony also reviewed the notes he had taken from speaking with Larry, which had helped him in the application phases at both departments. One thing hit him in the face that he had lost sight of on his first round of field training.

As Tony sat in this living room on a Sunday evening, prepping for his first day, he reviewed the notes he had written while talking to Larry two years prior. He found one that read, "Really ask yourself, is this a job or is this a career?" When he thought back on this conversation with Larry, he remembered Larry making the distinction that this career was something you needed passion to survive.

"If you don't have passion for this, it will eat you up. There is too much negative, and if you aren't in the right frame of mind, you won't survive it bro," echoed Larry's words.

With this guiding statement, Tony was determined to take a different approach to his training. Tony knew now that everything was on the line. A failure would financially set him back for years if he wasn't successful, and he had no intention of failing or quitting this time.

Tony decided his focus was going to be on good communication and sound tactics to help him engineer his success. As he continued to read through notes from Larry and from college, he wanted to solidify what his objectives were for training:

1. Find common ground with people, whether it's your trainer, others in the department or people on the street. This helps them to see your trustworthiness.

2. Learn to find things you like about people, and as you learn to like them, they'll learn to like you back in reciprocation.

3. Demonstrating humility to people is also another way of building trusting relationships. Don't be afraid to say you're sorry or to let people know you don't know everything.

4. Show people that you are interested in them. Exemplify a willingness to learn and listen to others and you will win them over more times than not.

5. Asking the good 'what' and 'how' questions, and then listening to the answers to truly understand his trainer and anyone he was talking to.

To avoid overwhelming himself initially, Tony focused on these five points to observe how they unfolded. Tony hadn't crossed paths with Thomas yet due to the latter being on vacation. The prospect of not knowing who Thomas was, given Tony's previous experience, made him a bit uneasy. On the first day, they finally met at the precinct. Since Tony wasn't yet a full-fledged officer, he hadn't been assigned a take-home vehicle. Upon Thomas's arrival, Tony noted his very short-cropped hair, sunglasses, and a clenched jaw that imparted an intense look. The department's rotating schedules meant officers shifted from day to swing, swing to grave, or grave back to day every three months. Fortunately, Tony had lucked out as Thomas had recently started his day shift schedule. Tony knew competing with sleep deprivation, in addition to his training, would have made things harder so he was happy for this lucky break.

As Thomas exited the car, Tony walked up and they shook hands, exchanging greetings. Thomas said, "There's not a lot of room, so I'll ask you to only bring what you absolutely need."

Tony looked at the car and noticed that even the back seat, where prisoners were transported, was full of equipment.

Thomas must have seen Tony's perturbed look and said, "Yeah, I know. I actually move the stuff to the trunk when we transport someone, because that bag has equipment that shouldn't be crushed down all the time."

Tony smiled and replied, "I am here to learn, sir. As long as we are safe, I will follow your lead."

Thomas said, "Sounds good, but knock off the sir stuff. You're a cop just like I was when I started. I am just here to teach you some stuff."

Tony felt a giant sense of relief and elation at these words. This was a much better start than last time. With all the excitement flowing through him he jogged back to his little Chevy pickup and grabbed a notepad and ticket book.

Tony then asked Thomas as he waved the notepad, "What are your thoughts on me taking notes about what I am learning from you?"

Tony, sticking to his plan, then shut up. He could see that Thomas might never have been asked that by a rookie, as he looked puzzled.

"I think it is a good idea, as long as you're not burying your nose in that notepad all the time."

Tony agreed and they were on their way. The first night on the job was pretty slow. Thomas, true to people's descriptions of him, was a very quiet guy. He didn't use the phone much, and was always looking for impaired drivers. Thomas explained that he had done a short stint with Highway Patrol during his career and really enjoyed D.U.I. investigations.

Tony noted that, literally, and then asked, "What makes you so passionate about D.U.I.'s?"

Tony learned that Thomas had seen early on that command staff and Sergeants always loved officers who took D.U.I. investigations seriously, and his focus on it had come from his trainer at Highway Patrol.

"Well I worked for Highway Patrol for a couple years and learned a lot about D.U.I.'s and took a lot of wrecks involving drunk and high drivers. It made me want to catch people before they hurt themselves or someone else when driving impaired," said Thomas.

Tony attentively listened to Thomas, jotting down notes that sparked further conversation. Before he knew it, Thomas was inquiring about Tony's departure from the large agency and the reasons behind choosing Little Green Valley. Tony approached the subject with caution, avoiding excessive negativity, and humbly explained his decision, emphasizing his readiness to work hard in the new setting.

Handling a couple of disturbance calls, a minor accident with no injuries, and a shoplifting incident at a convenience store, they concluded their shift. Tony completed the two reports he had, and Thomas returned them with some corrections, though not as severe as before. Tony breathed a sigh of relief while addressing the corrections. Held over for only about an hour, he headed home that night, expressing gratitude to God for the distinctly positive beginning to this new experience.

In his initial training week, Tony prioritized asking insightful questions, active listening, and conveying a sense of importance to both his trainer and the people on the street. However, establishing a connection with Thomas, who was a very private person, proved challenging. While Thomas had shared details about his happy marriage and three kids, it was still challenging to fully connect with him.

On the last day of the first week, Tony approached Thomas with a curious tone, asking what there was to do around the area. Surprisingly, Thomas opened up about ATV riding trails, sharing his enthusiasm for 'horn hunting' after deer shed their antlers. He delved into his rough ATV experiences and passion for hunting. Tony faced roadblocks in connecting due to financial constraints preventing him from owning an ATV and lacking experience in hunting. Despite this, he continued to listen attentively to understand more about Thomas.

Finally, a breakthrough emerged when Thomas revealed his fondness for running, describing himself as a 'slow and steady' type. Seizing the opportunity, Tony expressed his own love for running and sought Thomas's recommendations for trails.

The conversation took off from there as they discussed running and exercise. They paused the conversation for a burglary report they went to take, but as they broke for lunch at a local Mexican restaurant Thomas started, "So, the gym over here on the backside of the Walmart is a really good one if you want to meet up there someday."

Tony had really been getting to know and like Thomas already, but this was he and Tony's common ground. Eventually Thomas and another senior officer from the department would invite Tony to start running with them and working out. And it all started from just being genuinely curious about his trainer.

In the passing weeks, Tony came to the realization that he had retained more skills from his previous agency than he initially thought. He reflected on the idea that the knowledge acquired during his academy days seemed trapped in his mind, hindered by the stress that prevented him from accessing it fully. Training with Thomas felt like riding alongside a mentor, guiding him in the right direction.

On one call early in the training, Tony messed up on how he was handcuffing someone, and didn't get all the pertinent information from the victim that Thomas wanted him to. Tony felt a rush of anxiety which reminded him of his first training experience. Tony shut down, and Thomas obviously noticed.

Thomas pulled the car over to a gas station and said, "Hey, let's grab a soda."

As they walked out of the station, sodas in hand, Thomas stood at the front of the car with his reflective Oakley sunglasses on.

Tony thought he was about to get a lecture, so he cut it off at the pass, "I am sorry, I really screwed that up."

Thomas gave a big and rarely seen smile as he took a sip from his straw. "Yeah, you did," he said with a matter-of-fact tone.

Tony's head dropped, and just then Thomas said, "And that is what is supposed to happen. It would be weird if you didn't mess stuff up. My job is to take those mess-ups and help you learn from them."

Tony immediately felt better, and the two finished their drinks as they talked about what Tony had learned from that call.

As four months came to an end, Tony was in a position where he felt like he and Thomas were just partners, and he was the new guy taking the reports. Thomas had shown Tony a lot of respect in how he approached his mentoring and it had really worked.

Tony and Thomas sat down with their Sergeant who asked Tony, "So, what do you think, you ready to hit the street solo?"

Tony, in his normal way, responded that he humbly believed he was ready to challenge himself by being on his own and that

Thomas had put in a lot of work to prepare him. Tony then went back to a lesson he had learned before, the reversal. Tony inquired, "Sarge, how do you feel about me hitting the street on my own from what you have observed?"

The Sergeant smiled and said, "I think you are ready."

Thomas echoed the same, and just told Tony to stop getting lost on the way to calls.

The three of them laughed, and Tony said, "I promise to keep working on it."

Because Tony was a low man on the totem pole, he was going to one of the vacant spots the department had, which happened to be a graveyard shift position. He had never worked graveyards so he was curious what that would bring in the way of calls, but he was also excited because he would be working for Sergeant Tom Bartlett who he had met the night of his ride-along. Because it was a very small department, it would be Tony, Mark (who he had ridden with on his ride-along), and Sergeant Bartlett watching over the town at night.

Tony knew he still had a lot to learn, and he felt this was where he was meant to be in his first year. Over the next two years, Sergeant Bartlett would take Tony under his giant wing and teach him what a good cop was. Tony maintained the same rules and objectives as when he went into his field training and worked hard to make himself an asset to the department. This didn't mean Tony didn't mess things up and make mistakes, by sticking to his game plan he started to build a positive reputation as an officer.

Tony maintained a good relationship with Thomas and would continue to reach out to him for advice and guidance these first years. The two would try to get together to run and workout whenever they could, given their conflicting schedules. Equally as important, Tony developed a strong relationship with Sergeant Bartlett, who he would call 'Boss' for the rest of his life. Sergeant Bartlett had told him multiple times, "Antonio, call me Tom," but out of respect Tony couldn't bring himself to do that, so the middle ground for Tony was 'Boss'. Tony took a genuine interest in Sergeant Bartlett's experience and modeled his style of policing on what Sergeant Bartlett suggested and expected from his officers. As a result, Sergeant Bartlett was more than willing to invest in Tony.

One night, as Tony was diligently working on paperwork in his trusty old Chevy Caprice Interceptor, Sergeant Bartlett pulled up right beside him to check on him. In the quiet town, it wasn't uncommon for an officer to find some rest in their vehicle during the silent hours of the night. The officers often looked out for each other, ensuring no one was left in a vulnerable position. Tony had been learning valuable insights from Sergeant Bartlett since the beginning, and in the second week of his tenure on the squad, Tony took the opportunity to directly ask, "Boss, what do you believe defines a good officer?"

Sergeant Bartlett gave a slight smile and shifted the toothpick he always had in his mouth to the side. He then replied, "Okay, I see where you're going with this."

Tony replied, "No disrespect or trick, I promise. I am here to succeed, and I want to do the job right Boss."

Sergeant Bartlett shifted in his 1990's Chevy Blazer, which had been made into a patrol vehicle, most likely because the giant of a man couldn't fit in anything else. The whole Blazer would creak when he moved. Sergeant Bartlett looked out the windshield, then back at Tony and said, "What has helped me has to do with dignity."

Tony cocked his head, mostly because he was sleepy at 0400 and because he was trying to follow the logic. Sergeant Bartlett continued, "This might sound cheesy, but you asked me. I have found over the years that people are expecting officers to show up and be jerks. That being said, I have known a few jerk officers in my 25 years. So, I always tried to not be like those people. My goal has always been to show up, talk to people the way I would want my family members to be talked to. Most importantly, listen to what they have to say or their side of the story. I call it just visitin'."

Tony replied, "Visitin'?"

"Yeah," said Sergeant Bartlett, "people generally expect you to be badge-heavy with them, cause a lot of them have had that experience before. When you contact them and treat them like your 'visitin' with a new friend, it does something weird. I don't know exactly what it is, but all of a sudden, they are surprised you aren't what they expected you to be, and you earn a little bit of favor with them. It really goes a long way."

"Wow," said Tony as he rubbed his face, "that is wild that it works that way."

Sergeant Bartlett then said, "You keep that theme going by just inviting their story, make the conversation about them, not you. And you don't rush them. People want to tell you what happened and why they are calling the cops. You obviously aren't there on their best day, and they just want someone to listen to their story."

Tony then said, "I really like that Boss, but what Thomas taught me was not to let people drone on and on forever."

Sergeant Bartlett smiled, "Thomas is a great cop, no lie there, and you won't find many people who work as hard as him, however, I will say he could learn some more about communicating with people. What works for me in those 'droning' situations is trying to kindly redirect them to what led to today's issue, and if you have to cut them off, do it with some summarizing of what they were saying. Kind of like you are wrapping it up, by letting them know you understood what they were saying."

Tony listened intently as they continued talking, and he wrote down some notes. Sergeant Bartlett said, "You sure do take a lot of notes."

Tony chuckled and nodded 'yes' as he finished his thought on paper, which read, "Give people dignity in their bad times. Invite and listen to their stories and be willing to give them your time."

Tony and Sergeant Bartlett talked for a while longer about cop stuff, what it was like working in the big city and eventually transitioned to the topic of new trails to check out on their days off. As the sun started to peak over the hills just a bit, Sergeant Bartlett told Tony to head home and get rest. As Tony started up the old Caprice, Sergeant Bartlett began to pull away in his Blazer and hollered out his window, "And stop spilling coffee on your reports you turn in!"

Tony's first year was an amazing one of fun, experience, mistakes and even some good laughs. He was working closely with his partner Mark and getting to know everyone around the department. He was so excited to be there that every day felt like an adventure as opposed to a workday. There were some interesting characters in the department, and Tony's excitement rubbed some of them the wrong way. The guy that had been hired by the department just prior to Tony was named Juan.

Juan had a bad attitude and had transferred off of Sergeant Bartlett's squad just before Tony was hired. He had come from another agency and apparently brought his poor attitude with him. Every time Tony would run into Juan on the street, Juan would tell him he wasted too much time talking to people and needed to stop being so involved. Tony had learned to ignore Juan, but his bad attitude still bothered Tony at times. One night in particular, as Tony was finishing some paperwork in the briefing room, Juan started in on him, mocking that he had taken several reports that Juan felt could have been avoided. As Tony sat smiling and just letting Juan's comments roll off his back, the department traffic investigator Officer Dwyer walked into the briefing room.

Officer Dwyer was a legend in the department. He had survived a 25-year career in the big agency that Tony had quit from, and came to the department immediately after retiring as a Sergeant from the Air Unit of the big agency. This was all several years before Tony had started with Little Green Valley. Officer Dwyer had only been at Little Green Valley P.D. for about two years when he responded to a report of disturbance at the local Walmart. When he arrived at the disturbance call, he was confronted by a man with a gun. As the man and Officer Dwyer struggled over the suspect's gun, Officer Dwyer was able to get his pistol out and fire a single shot. Unfortunately, because of the close contact, the slide on Officer Dwyer's gun couldn't fully cycle and his weapon jammed after he had gotten a single shot off. As the altercation went on, Officer Dwyer suffered two handgun shots to the abdomen but was able to get his bearings, surviving until other officers arrived to help take the suspect into custody. It was a long recovery after the incident, but Officer Dwyer survived and even came back to work as the traffic officer after that. He was a real life John Wayne.

Tony rolled with the punches as Juan was giving him a hard time that night in the briefing room, and he just continued doing what he was doing at the computer. Officer Dwyer, who was usually quiet, found a pause in Juan's rant.

He then started, "I gotta' tell you Antonio, after what I have seen on some calls with you, and hearing how you talk to people, I am impressed."

Juan scoffed and Tony smiled and humbly said, "Thank you."

Officer Dwyer continued, "All I have to say is whatever the other department didn't see in you, I am glad we ended up with you."

Juan laughed sarcastically and stormed out of the building. Officer Dwyer flashed Tony a wink and a smile, and then walked out of the room. Tony couldn't help but notice that all he had learned along the way was helping him become the officer he had always hoped to be and that was a huge accomplishment for Tony.

Around a year into his tenure at the department, Sergeant Bartlett successfully persuaded Tony to invest in an ATV, leading to their regular outings for hours on their days off, usually once or twice a week. During these rides, Tony discovered Sergeant Bartlett's extensive knowledge of the area and its history, which he found highly enjoyable. However, what captivated Tony even more was Sergeant Bartlett's profound understanding of people.

Sergeant Bartlett possessed a unique ability to connect with individuals, always allowing those involved in their calls to establish the tone for the interaction. Even though he was accustomed to being the 'Boss,' Sgt. Bartlett would even respectfully address people exhibiting initial poor behavior, providing them with an opportunity to reset the conversation with respect. This approach had a remarkable effect, keeping people calm and creating a sense of confusion, prompting them to eventually respond with respect. To Tony, it seemed like magic.

One chilly January night about two and a half years into Tony's time at Little Green Valley, Sergeant Bartlett had responded with Tony and one of his trainees to a report of a suspicious subject behind a gas station. The clerks had called 911 after hearing a loud noise on the backside of the building. As the officers crept around towards the alley behind the gas station, there sat a naked man sitting on a large rock and sweating profusely. It was

27 degrees outside. Sergeant Bartlett was quarterbacking the call and turned to Tony and his trainee.

Sergeant Bartlett said, "Listen, this guy is really wigged out. Don't know what he is on today, but this is not a good situation."

Sergeant Bartlett then positioned Tony and his trainee in the wooded area to the east, making an 'L' formation. Sergeant Bartlett stayed at the corner of the building, about 35 feet away from the man. As they got in place Sergeant Bartlett started communicating, "Scott, this is Tom Bartlett." The man's head perked up and he looked over to Sergeant Bartlett who obviously knew the man.

"Scott, you look lost. How can I help you?"

The man yelled out, "Screw you man!"

Scott then grabbed a glass bottle that was next to him and shattered it against the rock he was seated on. He held it up towards Sergeant Bartlett, indicating that no one should approach him, but he didn't get up. Solid as a giant rock, Sergeant Bartlett moved ever so slightly, using the building for a little more cover, and had his hand on his gun, ready to break leather in the case that Scott charged him.

The Sergeant then said, "You seem really pissed Scott. What happened tonight?"

Scott went on an angry tirade about his wife kicking him out. "...Because she is a selfish bitch. Ya I am pissed!" Scott also said something about his in-laws and kids hating him.

Sergeant Bartlett then followed, "So, it sounds like you have a ton of pressure at home, a bunch of people who are disrespecting you and nowhere to go."

Scott sarcastically replied, "Well whoopty doo big guy! You figured my life out."

Sergeant Bartlett rolled with the sarcasm, his calm tone never changing. "My only concern is helping you right now. It is cold out, you don't have any clothes on, and even though you feel fine right now, you are going to end up freezing out here."

What followed was another tirade and a few more outbursts. Sergeant Bartlett didn't rush Scott, nor did he ever use his size or authority to intimidate him. He simply would ask a question, stay quiet when Scott responded and then rephrase what Scott had said to show he understood him. Sometimes Sergeant Bartlett would even just sit in silence with Scott, and Scott would go off on a tangent to break the silence. It took about an hour, but Scott eventually wore himself out, and was convinced to get into an ambulance and head to the hospital. Tony was always impressed with Sergeant Bartlett, but tonight was especially extraordinary.

After the call, as they stood in front of their cars at a gas station, Tony asked, "Boss, how do you do that? How do you always calm these people down?"

Sergeant Bartlett shifted the toothpick in his mouth and adjusted his gun belt as he leaned on his patrol vehicle.

"You know, a few things come to mind. The first thing I have always shared with you is that you have to give people their dignity. Even a man lying in the gutter deserves his dignity, and if they perceive you are taking it from them, well, be ready for a fight."

Tony nodded his head, and asked his rookie if he was taking notes. The young officer quickly took out his tiny notebook and started to write.

Sergeant Bartlett then added, "I also learned a long time ago from reading a lot that you have to bear in mind the hero's struggle."

"The hero's struggle? You have never mentioned this one to me," replied Tony.

"Yeah, it is like a shortcut to empathy for me. A lot of people have all these deep and descriptive ways of describing empathy nowadays, but this is my shortcut," shared the Sergeant. "The vast majority of human beings have what I have heard people call 'main character energy.' We all believe we are the hero of the story, when in reality, I am 'police sergeant #1', or just 'the big dude standing at the check-out aisle in a grocery store' in another person's story. Everyone believes they are the main character. The problem is that when you come to a call-for-service, you have to understand that the moment you try to be the hero or simply don't let them be the hero, you run the risk of becoming the *villain* in the other person's story. This makes for a lot of negative emotions on their part. The easiest way to open communication and demonstrate empathy is letting the person you are talking to be the hero in the story and make it your job to hear their story. If you can do this then you become an ally to the hero and they will be more willing to work with you, hear you out."

"That is incredible, Boss. I love it. I have been doing this all so wrong," said Tony.

"The last thing that always works for me is coming to the table with a blank slate."

"Meaning what, boss?" asked Tony.

"Well, I am the big giant cop everyone knows, right? But people knew me even before I wore the badge. I have grown up in this town, and everyone has their impressions of me. Small towns are like that. Once you get a reputation here, it follows you for the rest of your life. Hard to shake, and I am no different than anyone else in that regard. So, when I come to them and treat them like I have no judgements about them or preconceived notion about who I am talking to, other than their name if I know it, then people tend to listen a little bit more. I give them a fair shake every time."

Tony looked at his trainee and said, "I highly suggest you learn as much as you can from boss, if you want to be successful out here."

Sergeant Bartlett then turned towards the trainee and added, "This goes along the lines of what I have told Tony before. People always expect officers to be badge heavy. When you come to them with something different and listen to them, it shakes them and then you can reframe the entire interaction and conversation. It opens up a world of possibilities."

Tony thanked the Sergeant for all the advice, and then turned to his trainee, "We have reports to get done if you want to get home on time. So, we are going to head to the office, boss."

Sergeant Bartlett nodded, and said, "Catch you guys later."

CHAPTER 8

THE PHOENIX

It had been seven good years since Tony started with Little Green Valley P.D., and he had gained a lot experience and stories, including bar fights, countless drunk people, death investigations, barricades, suicides, suspects resisting arrest, and even an attempted homicide on Tony and several of his colleagues one freezing cold February night. Tony had survived all these situations by the grace of God, and he had built great relationships along the way. Starting with Sergeant Bartlett's mentoring, Tony had been offered and taken opportunities to be a field training officer, a member of the small S.W.A.T. team for the region, a firearms instructor, defensive tactics instructor and a co-chair for a committee that put on a community policing-based carnival every year.

The department had afforded Tony a lot of chances for experience, and although Sergeant Bartlett had retired three years into Tony's career, the Sergeant had mentored Tony into a decent hard-working officer in that time. It was hard for Tony when Sergeant Bartlett retired, because he had learned so much from him, and because they had become quite close.

After the "boss" left, Tony kept pushing forward though it wasn't the same. In his fifth year, Tony embraced a considerable amount of responsibility, having trained a total of 10 new officers, served as an instructor in various areas, all while continuing his work on the streets. Every moment spent serving the small community brought him immense joy. Tony couldn't ignore the fact that choosing to come to Little Green Valley had proven to be an excellent decision for him.

Tony had recently accepted a position as a Detective at the P.D. He had been looking for a challenge when he tested for the investigation spot. It was something different, but Tony wasn't quite sure if he liked it. In the smaller jurisdiction, detectives handled everything from burglaries to homicides and everything in between. It was a big difference from patrol work and Tony couldn't stand being in the office every day. He would look out the window of his office and sorely missed being in his patrol Tahoe, cruising around. Tony looked for every opportunity to go out to interview people and collect evidence when he could so that he wouldn't feel so trapped.

One night, during the late hours, Tony found himself alone in his office, glancing at the additional folding table he had set up just two days ago to organize grocery bags filled with prescription pills. The station was peaceful, and Tony appreciated the quiet, especially since he disliked the daytime office shift due to its many distractions. His current focus was on a commercial burglary that occurred the previous week. Fortunately, his reputation in the small town had prompted an anonymous caller to provide him with valuable information about the suspects involved in the case.

Tony had worked with the anonymous caller and was able to recover the majority of the prescription drugs stolen from the pharmacy and make two arrests associated with the burglary and drugs. Now he needed to separate all the different drugs to classify them for further charges to be filed on the suspects. This was a daunting task, but he knew what he would be doing for the next few days. Tony felt a sense of accomplishment for having closed the burglary case with an arrest, but the position still wasn't what he thought it was going to be. A very unfortunate part of taking the detective position was that Tony was working with a weasel of an officer who he couldn't stand. This 'Detective' was well known for his laziness, talking down to people and being a jerk in general. It was hard for Tony to say anything since he was the new guy in the position, but just having an office next to the guy was demoralizing.

To add to his daily stress, Tony was going through a divorce. Tony had met a young woman who worked as a dispatcher for Little Green Valley P.D. a year after he started working there. They quickly grew fond of each other and had moved in together within the year of meeting. A year after that the two were married. Tony had initially believed that the two had a lot in common, but after they were married Tony realized that it was the law enforcement connection that made Tony feel that strong sense of closeness. The relationship eventually grew cold, even after Tony's wife had their son Enzo. Tony struggled with the decision to walk away from the marriage, but he thought it might be easier on his son if the marriage ended before the little guy could remember Tony and his wife being together.

Tony's soon to be ex-wife had grown up in Little Green Valley, and Tony was feeling a lot of pressure surrounding the separation from people in the community and department because Tony was the outsider. The divorce was fueled by a significant disagreement – Tony's desire to move back to the big city. He expressed concerns about limited professional growth and dismal wages in Little Green Valley, along with worries about their son's educational opportunities. Unfortunately, Tony's wife adamantly refused to discuss leaving the small community, leading to considerable tension. Tony struggled to find motivation to stay in Little Green Valley as the challenges between him and his wife mounted.

One morning after Tony had separated from his wife, he dropped little Enzo off at daycare. Tony then went back to his guest house to relax before getting ready for work. Tony was lucky to have found a small home to rent from a nice, retired couple during the separation. It was perfect for him and Enzo with a low ceiling, a small kitchen, a living room, and two tiny bedrooms separated by a small bathroom. The tiny house was tucked away into a nice, quiet neighborhood where they would rarely even see cars drive by.

Tony sat down on his porch sipping some coffee, enjoying the views of the mountains on the late winter morning. The scene was a serenely quiet one. A light breeze cut through the juniper trees, and he felt relaxed by the whisper of the breeze through the branches. As he sat there his mind wandered, kind of wallowing in the negativity of his personal and professional situation. Tony took responsibility for his own part in the mess, but he also wondered what his life would be like had he not fallen to the pressure of his first trainer. He might have been a supervisor by now or doing something even more interesting.

It had always eaten at Tony that he wasn't successful in the big city as an officer, no matter how many accolades or extra opportunities came his way. This constant thought made him feel like he was always going to be an impostor as an officer no matter how much responsibility he took on at Little Green Valley. This was one of the reasons Tony wanted to move back to the city, to prove to himself he could make it. As he sipped his coffee, a sense of purpose came over him and he thought to himself, *I wonder what would happen if I reapplied to my old agency.*

Tony really liked the thought the more he ruminated on it. He decided he would send Larry an email. Although Tony hadn't spoken with Larry in years, he figured if nothing else it would be nice to catch up. Tony sent the email off and then went out for a run before he reported to the office for the day.

A week went by, and Tony had gotten busy with investigations and had all but forgotten about the email to Larry. Life was especially busy for Tony on the days that he had little Enzo, so it was easy to forget things. Even though the divorce was not cordial, Tony and his soon-to-be ex-wife had decided to split time with Enzo 50/50. This kept Tony busy, but he didn't mind it one bit. He loved being a dad. When he wasn't with Enzo, Tony tried to stay busy working or working out. As Tony was getting ready for his shift one morning, his cell phone rang.

He put his coffee down on the counter, answered the phone and then, "Brooooooooooooo!!!!!!" said the voice on the other end of the line.

"Larry!" said Tony, "how the hell are you?"

What followed was a conversation years in the making. Both Larry and Tony had a lot to catch up on. Larry was now working in the Community Engagement Bureau at Tony's previous police department and he was doing very well. He was running the police volunteer program and having a great time. Larry sounded as happy as Tony had ever heard him, and it was contagious. Tony definitely needed a little bit of energy at that moment. Larry had plenty of questions for Tony that made Tony feel like he really mattered. Tony shared what had been going on professionally and then went into sharing about the divorce.

Larry listened and when he had a chance, he asked, "Brother, what can I do to help?"

Tony hated asking for help, so he started with, "I think I'll be good, man. Just have to let some time pass and hope things cool down." As he finished that statement Tony felt a twinge inside his chest and then blurted out, "What do you think the odds would be of me coming back?"

Larry answered, "Dude, I would move mountains to make it happen. Let me reach out to my buddy who is the Lieutenant in hiring and pave that path."

Tony expressed his great appreciation to Larry.

Larry then said, "Hey man, I know you are solid, but just give me a heads up with the reason you are trying to leave. You know the people above always ask."

Knowing what Larry was getting at, Tony replied, "It is honestly just the divorce and the pressures surrounding that man. No discipline pending, no open investigations or anything."

"Cool man, that is easy to work with," said Larry in an upbeat tone.

Tony then added, "And man, the other thing is, I hate that I quit. It has been eating at me since I left. This is a way for me to prove I can do it."

Larry then shared with Tony that he knew it was a hard decision when Tony made it, but really what mattered is that it had led to this point, and Larry was excited to help make this happen for Tony.

As they ended the phone call Larry told Tony, "We got this man. We can get you out of there and on a better path soon, just give me some time to work on some things."

With that, Tony hung up and he felt a rush of endorphins that made him feel lightheaded. He couldn't believe this might be happening. Tony put on his shoes, grabbed his coffee and felt as if he was walking on a cloud as he headed out the door to start his day.

Tony didn't hear from Larry for a few weeks, and the thought lingered in his mind that the previous department didn't want him back. Tony tried to push that negative thought away and focused on time with his son and his duties as a detective. At this point, Tony had stepped down from his position on the regional tactical team. It had become too hard to feel safe during operations. His soon-to-be ex-brother-in-law was one of the senior members of the team and had made it very uncomfortable for Tony because of the pending divorce. Tony felt walls closing around him at the department and he handled the stress by taking his boy out to hike and camp in the area every weekend he had him.

One Sunday afternoon, Tony had taken Enzo to a nearby creek to enjoy the cool air, shade, and fragrant aroma of the pine trees while they picnicked and played in the water. It was a perfect afternoon and little Enzo was having the time of his life in the cool creek. At one point the two even fell asleep on a blanket, under the shade of a beautiful, tall ponderosa. As the sun dipped behind the rim of the canyon the temperature dropped quickly. Little Enzo ran up shivering, and Tony wrapped him in a towel. Tony put Enzo in the SUV, securing the little guy in his car seat. As Tony made his third trip to the car with the camp chairs, he noticed Enzo had fallen into a deep sleep like only toddlers can do. Tony finished packing and slowly drove out of the small parking lot by the creek back towards town.

As Tony merged onto the highway from the side road, his phone buzzed with a voicemail notification. He wondered if it was a work-related call, considering the occasional pressure from his supervisor to come in on days off, a common drawback of being a detective in a small town. Attempting to listen to the message, Tony found the signal too weak, making it impossible to discern the content or the caller. Deciding not to stress about it, he opted for a Kenny Chesney album, enjoying the 30-minute drive back into town while Enzo napped in the back seat. Upon arriving home, Tony woke up Enzo, settled him with a movie and popcorn, and headed to the small kitchen. Retrieving a frozen glass from the freezer, he poured himself a whiskey on ice before stepping outside onto the porch. Seated in an Adirondack-style chair, he took a sip and called his voicemail. The message was from Larry.

"Hey bro, I know you are probably spending time with Enzo. Just wanted to let you know the good news that your application is on the fast-track, and you'll be hearing from them this week. I think it will be Michelle reaching out to you. She and I are old pals, so I have given her the heads up on your situation. Call me tomorrow morning."

Tony was thrilled to hear this. As he sat smiling, he took another sip of the sour mash whiskey and reminded himself that this was just the beginning. There were still several hills to climb, and any one of those hills could derail the process. This was no time for a full-on celebration. Tony then started to think about the complications that would go with living in the big city without Enzo. He didn't know how this would all look, or how much time he would have with his boy. His heart raced, and he felt pressure in his chest, as if his heartbeats were stronger now. Tony's excitement was officially stifled and a dark feeling creeped over him, that would never quite go away from that point on.

The hiring process went as well as could be expected. With Larry's help, there were no snags along the way. In reality, Tony received a warm welcome and numerous apologies from colleagues at the department for the mistreatment he had endured years ago. It really felt like a homecoming. As the hiring date drew near, Tony arranged to meet Larry for lunch on a sunny afternoon in May.

As they sat catching up and having a cold beer, Larry said, "Dude! I forgot to tell you."

Tony looked at Larry with a raise of his eyebrows.

Larry continued, "Bro, so Leslie, your old trainer, was just put on suspension."

Tony sarcastically replied, "What? That is wild, can't imagine for what," then took a big drink of his beer.

Larry then added, "So, I guess it was a situation with some mentally ill person, who had threatened suicide. Leslie showed up as the Sergeant on scene and rushed the whole situation because he and his people 'didn't have time for this crap.' I don't know all the details, but Leslie ended up shooting the guy and the department is *not* happy with how it played out. As a result, the family of the man and community are in an uproar about it, and he is looking at a demotion."

Tony was shocked that the man had been promoted in the first place, but he also knew from experience how tough an internal investigation could be for officers. "Did the person die?" asked Tony.

Larry replied, "Yeah dude, the guy didn't make it. That is why the family is so upset."

Tony then said, "Well, I don't care for that guy, and he treated me like crap, but I don't wish him ill either. Sorry to hear about that tragedy."

Larry smiled, "That's legit, bro. Good karma on you."

They both raised their glasses, 'clinked' them together and took a big swig as their meals were delivered to the table.

*   *   *

The first day at the new precinct was interesting to say the least. Tony hadn't been able to find a place to stay yet, so he was staying with his tía at her house on the days he worked. She had been gone, traveling for work for many years as an assistant to a politician in Texas at one point and as customer service manager in Colorado, but was now back in the city living in a very centralized location. Tony's tía had been very important to him since he had been in diapers, and he was really happy she would now be around for Enzo too. She was quick to offer Tony a place to stay when she found out he had taken the new job.

Tony had left her house early in the day for his swing shift. He had been assigned to work in the same precinct he worked in when he left the department, but the city had built a new building that was very nice. Tony pulled into the facility and brought in his uniform that he kept in a travel bag, along with his equipment. He walked into the new locker room and picked out one of the empty lockers. He hung his things up and then went into the workout room to get out some of his jitters. Tony had met his new Field Training Officer the week before, a short muscular guy named Todd. Todd was quiet but nice enough at their first meeting; still, Tony really didn't know what to expect.

Tony finished out his cardio routine on the elliptical trainer and showered up. As he got ready, he couldn't help but feel like something was off. Tony finished getting dressed and walked into the hallway. As he looked towards the briefing room, he could see a Lieutenant standing at the door. Tony couldn't remember his name, but he remembered meeting this Lieutenant years before when he was an officer who was training Tony's class of recruits at the academy. Tony hated forgetting people's names, recognizing the significance of remembering someone's name in creating a favorable impression. As Tony approached the door, he extended his hand out for a handshake to the Lieutenant and in a friendly voice said, "Afternoon, sir."

The Lieutenant smiled and said, "You must be the new guy."

Tony answered, "Yes sir, just happy to be here and be given the opportunity."

The Lieutenant then replied, "I guess they don't wear badges where you come from, Mr. New guy," then pointed at Tony's chest.

Tony's face flushed full of blood, and he grabbed at where his badge should have been. He felt the empty spot and started to panic.

"I am sorry, sir," he blurted out. "I will find it."

Tony hustled back to the locker room and searched and searched and searched. He then ran out to his SUV. He tore the car apart but could not find his badge. He couldn't believe this was happening.

Tony made his way back into the briefing room, and Todd, who had been apprised of what was going on dryly said, "I hope you found it."

Tony had learned that being open, honest, and forthright about bad news was the best policy, so he replied, "I really screwed up, Todd. I must have left it at home when I was getting things ready."

As Tony said this, he thought to himself about where he possibly could have left the badge. He was very meticulous the night before in getting his uniform ready, and hadn't remembered taking the badge off the pressed shirt.

Todd shook his head and was about to say something when a kind voice called out from the front of the room, "I got you."

A tall female officer with her hair in two little buns on the top of her head walked up to Tony and said, "Hey, I'm Katie." She shook Tony's hand firmly, "I have an extra badge for you to borrow. Follow me." Tony walked with Katie into the hallway, and she asked, "You're the guy from Little Green Valley, right?"

Tony, who was completely distraught at this point, answered, "Yeah, just got back here."

Katie said, "That's cool. Hold on a sec while I grab that from my locker."

Tony waited for a few nervous minutes and Katie returned with the badge. He thanked her and they walked into the briefing together. After briefing, Todd and Tony hit the street. Todd didn't make a big deal about the badge, nor did he give Tony a long speech. They just started going to calls for service together. As they went from call to call, Tony got the impression that Todd was just trying to make sure Tony knew what he was doing. Tony jumped in as primary officer on every call that day and just needed Todd's help in finding his way through some of the neighborhoods. He also needed Todd's help with the booking process when they arrested a suspect with a misdemeanor warrant. As they wrapped up the shift, Tony finished a couple of reports he had taken, and Todd asked him to make a couple of corrections.

Tony wrapped up the night and handed the badge back to Katie when she walked by. He thanked her, and she said, "No problem, 'Little Green', stuff happens."

Tony looked at her with a questioning look. Katie smiled and said, "I'm calling you 'Little Green' from now on. Deal with it," and she walked away.

As Tony was getting dressed down in the locker room, he heard a 'thunk' sound when he put down his shirt. He picked the shirt back up. In the fold of one of the alterations that the seamstress had made was the badge. It had somehow come unpinned and fallen in there. With the stress of the first day combined with the thick weight of the ballistic vest, Tony hadn't felt the badge in there at any point during his shift. He had to laugh to himself and pinned the badge back on the shirt before he hung it up. Tomorrow would be a new day and he knew exactly where his badge was.

CHAPTER 9

CONNECTING IN CRISIS

Tony had been working graveyards for over a year in the big city. It had been a rough first year with the lack of sleep and driving back and forth to get Enzo from Little Green Valley every week, but he was making it work for them. The transition from the small town back to the big city was not bad at all for Tony. He was pleasantly surprised that his biggest struggle was just getting used to finding his way around the neighborhoods in his beat area.

He had a decent squad and he had become close with one of his squadmates who everyone called 'Fish' (short for Fisher). A rookie officer, Fish was a good dude, just kind of goofy, but a hard worker. He and Tony hit it off early on and they liked rolling into calls together. Another thing Tony had to get adjusted to was the fact that there was rarely dead time, even on a graveyard shift in the big city. It was as if the normal-ish people would go to bed around 2200 hours, but after midnight a whole different culture of people woke up and wandered the streets, causing all kinds of havoc. Tony just couldn't believe the amount of activity there was. The good thing was that it kept him wide awake, and he always had good stories to tell at the end of the week.

Tony and Fish were working for another giant of a man who went by the name Mark Pine, on his graveyard squad. Mark was a no-nonsense type of Sergeant who was tactically as smart as they come. He was also a hulk and looked a lot like Michael Clark Duncan from the movie "The Green Mile." Tony always responded well to strong leadership and Sergeant Pine was just the type of supervisor that he liked working for.

One hot May evening, a 911 call came in from a military veteran who was calmly requesting police respond to his house. The man told the dispatcher that he had a rifle, was ready to die, and wanted officers to be the ones to kill him. Then, he hung up. On the return call from dispatch, he would not answer the phone. Sergeant Pine told everyone responding to meet about 100 yards up the street from the caller's location. Dispatch sent a message on the mobile data terminal to all responding officers that the caller's demeanor and tone were eerily ice cold during the call with the 911 operator. It had left the operator a bit shaken.

As the officers on Tony's squad arrived, Sergeant Pine advised that he had a plan and started to hand out assignments to officers. Tony was hoping that Sergeant Pine would assign him to cover the front of the home with his rifle, but that wasn't the plan. Sergeant Pine advised that he needed Tony to make a phone call to the veteran, to see if he could effectively communicate with him. Tony was surprised, but his assignment was to make the call. Tony set up in his car with Sergeant Pine's work cell phone, and once everyone was surrounding the house, it was time for Tony to make the call.

"Who the fuck is this?" answered the man on the line.

"Hey, my name is Antonio," said Tony nervously.

"Well Alfonso, I'll take two bean burritos to go!" yelled the man before he hung up. Tony looked at Sergeant Pine, who was standing outside the driver's side window of the police Tahoe.

"Alright man, try it again, he sounds drunk, so we'll just have to work through that layer."

Tony dialed the number again.

"Do you got my burritos, Alfonz?" said the man mockingly.

"I am sorry," said Tony. "My name is Antonio, and I am a police officer outside of your home."

"Alfonz, so they sent you to kill me, did they?"

Tony replied, "I am not here to kill anyone."

"Well, you are here to protect AND serve, so I need someone to serve me by putting me out of my misery," he slurred.

"Sir, I don't know all that happened, and I won't pretend to understand, however, I will say that I am here to help."

"Well, ain't that cute!" yelled the man and hung up the phone again.

Tony realized he didn't really know what he was doing or how he was going to help this very angry man. Sergeant Pine keyed up his radio and let the other officers around the house know what was going on.

He then turned to Tony, "Hey man, you're doing good. Take some deep breaths and call him again. Just keep doing what you're doing."

Tony took that deep breath and called the phone number again. No answer. Tony dialed again, no answer. The third attempt finally yielded an answer.

"What the fuck, just send me someone with some balls to do the job!" the man yelled.

Tony stayed silent.

The man yelled, "Well, you sending someone to do this or not?!"

Tony stayed quiet, not for any reason other than being nervous. "Talkative one, ain't ya," said the man, mockingly.

"I am sorry sir, just trying to let you vent," replied Tony, adding, "what happened to get you to this point sir?"

From that point on, Tony had the gentleman hooked. Once Tony was able to start asking quality questions, the man went into venting. He shared with Tony that his name was David and he suffered from chronic pain. David had apparently been a high school baseball star, who blew his pitching arm out, so he ended up in the Army. David talked for a bit about what a great ball player he had been and how unfair life was. Tony sat with him on that for a while, letting him get out his anger. David began to cry. He then went on a tangent about his family not supporting him. Tony, remembering what Sergeant Bartlett had taught him, paraphrased what he had heard about David's family and then said, "How does that tie into today, David?"

This was just enough to get David back on track. He then started on that day's issue. David told Tony he had gotten hurt in boot camp about five years ago and hurt his back. He then went on to say that he had gotten addicted to prescription pain meds after being discharged from the military for his back injury. Tony apologized for this having been David's experience. At that moment in the conversation an officer on the perimeter of the home accidentally hit his flashlight and shined into a window of the home. Up to this point David didn't know the house had been surrounded. That's when David heated back up.

"You lying piece of shit, I knew you were coming to kill me! You are worthless and a liar to boot!" screamed David along with some racial slurs, then hung up the phone.

Just then Tony felt Sergeant Pine's strong grip on his left arm. Tony looked at him and he quietly mouthed, "Stay chill. Don't take that bait."

Tony took some deep breaths as Sergeant Pine cleared over the radio to update the perimeter officers. He dialed the phone number again.

"Jesus Christ you moron! Send your people in here and get the job done!" yelled David.

Tony replied calmly, "David, I explained what our goals are here today, and you and I will be shaking hands at some point."

This seemed to defuse David's angry barbs. As the conversation continued for another hour Tony did his best to just maintain calm and keep David focused. At one point David and Tony were just talking, and David said, "Alright man, what do you need me to do?"

Tony explained the exit plan to David, and he had some questions. He then bought himself some more time by venting more. Tony paraphrased what David said again to get him back on track. After about 10 more minutes of 'putting on his socks and shoes' he came out of the home and walked down the street to where David and Sergeant Pine were standing. David was a tall, thin young man in his 20's. It looked like David hadn't shaved or changed his clothes in weeks. David moved slowly towards Tony, and he looked nervously around as he did so. The perimeter officers had maintained concealment and stayed in place so as not to scare David.

Much to Tony's concern, David walked out of his house with a giant behemoth of a bull mastiff next to him, off-leash. Tony happened to be terrified of dogs and this situation made him very nervous. As a patrol officer Tony had been bitten twice by dogs while on calls and had another near miss with two mastiff's early in his career. He often wondered if he smelled like a giant dog treat to dogs.

True to Tony's word, Tony and David shook hands and they continued to talk. Sergeant Pine stepped back a few steps and was letting the others know what was going on, and the plan if David didn't comply. Tony, after learning about David's suicidal statements, insisted on taking him to a medical facility for evaluation. However, David adamantly refused, claiming it was not part of their agreement. In an attempt to escape, David bolted back towards his residence.

Suddenly, two officers emerged from the shadows, deploying a stun bag shotgun to halt David in his driveway. The loud but non-lethal tool achieved its purpose, causing momentary incapacitation and allowing for David's detention. After the fire department staff checked David for any injuries, Tony told Sergeant Pine that he would transport David into the emergent mental health facility, but Sergeant Pine said, "Nah, I'll have someone else take him. You pulled more than your weight on that."

After the call, Sergeant Pine debriefed with all the officers on scene. Everyone had done a great job maintaining their positions, showing patience and discipline, and eventually taking the subject into custody without any real injury. Sergeant Pine then mentioned that he was particularly thankful that Tony had taken the time to talk with someone who was very difficult to work with, maybe even saving David's life.

"Man, you never know with these folks. He was asking us to kill him. We didn't give that to him, and you bought enough trust with him to get him out of the house so we could detain him and get him some much needed help. It was a positive result," remarked Sergeant Pine as he closed out the debrief.

Tony started to walk back towards his vehicle and Sergeant Pine called to him, "Hey man! You look upset."

Tony turned back, "Sorry Sarge, just mad at myself that I didn't grab him up when he ran."

Sergeant Pine flashed a big smile then said, "Oh that?! C'mon man! Your head was in the world of communication. I didn't expect you to transition that fast. Communicating with someone in a crisis makes it difficult to transition into tactical mode. Plus, what were you supposed to do? Get bitten by that bear that came out with him? That's why I had a contingency plan set up. It was all teamwork, and you did your part just right. I trusted you and I also trusted the team to do what they had to."

Tony felt a little bit better and thanked Sergeant Pine as he hopped into his Tahoe.

Tony had found a surprising rush in communicating with someone in crisis. He knew that those calls were few and far between, but he did enjoy the idea of helping someone on one of the worst days of their life. This thought sat with him for several weeks after the call. One of those nights a few weeks later, Tony was sitting in his Tahoe, going through some training videos on his mobile data terminal when he opened up his work email. As he looked at the emails, one in particular caught his eye. It was for Crisis Intervention Training being offered by the department. Tony forwarded the email to Sergeant Pine, asking what he thought about Tony attending. Sergeant Pine replied before the end of shift with a very positive and encouraging tone. Tony sent his request to take the class and signed off shift for the night.

That following Monday, Tony started his last shift of the week and checked his email. He read a reply correspondence in reference to the Crisis Intervention Training (C.I.T.) which let him know the class was full, but he was on a waiting list for the next class being offered in three months. It wasn't great news, but at least he had made the list.

Three months later, Tony successfully enrolled in the C.I.T. (Crisis Intervention Training) course. Throughout the week of instruction, he found the curriculum to be engaging. The program covered various aspects, including recognizing specific mental health conditions at the street level and understanding how to handle such interactions effectively. Another significant part of the course focused on informing officers about available resources for individuals facing mental health challenges.

The segment that intrigued Tony the most delved into a set of verbal de-escalation tactics known as Active Listening Skills (A.L.S.). Though he couldn't pinpoint where he had encountered these skills before, they felt strangely familiar.

The Active Listening Skills that were covered started with little things called minimal encouragers. These were things people do in communication like nodding their heads or saying 'yeah' or 'uhu'. The next topic covered was something Tony was already familiar with and frequently utilized—open-ended questions. Tony had a strong preference for using questions in the form of 'what' or 'how,' and he found considerable success employing this style. Following that, the course introduced the skill of reflections, a concept that Tony was particularly fond of. Reflecting, as Tony discovered in the class, involved taking the last few words of a statement or key words from the last phrase someone uttered, demonstrating active listening. The class emphasized that people appreciate hearing their words repeated to them, and it can contribute to a positive feeling, fostering a stronger connection. Tony became increasingly intrigued as he delved into the art of active listening, furiously scribbling notes in his notebook.

The subsequent skills covered emotional labeling, paraphrasing, 'I' statements, and summarizing. Tony had encountered paraphrasing before through Sergeant Bartlett, finding it relatively straightforward. Summarizing, a more elaborate version of paraphrasing, involved encapsulating more details and information, serving as effective tools to guide or conclude a conversation. On the other hand, 'I' statements struck Tony as somewhat cheesy, and he initially wasn't a fan. However, upon further exploration, Tony discovered that 'I' statements originated from the therapeutic realm and, when employed with the right tone and context, could be a subtle yet effective way to address confrontational situations.

For instance, Tony learned about using an 'I' statement when someone engaged in dangerous behavior, such as waving a knife. In such a scenario, he could express concern by saying, "I get really worried about you when you start raising that knife because I don't want you to get hurt." Tony recognized the value of this approach but understood the importance of using it judiciously to avoid making the conversation about himself.

What Tony found extremely formidable as a communication tactic later in his career was the emotional label. Emotional labeling is the identification of your counterpart's feelings in a situation you are discussing. Tony learned that when it comes to emotional labeling, it isn't enough to just tell people, "You sound angry," or "Seems like you are really sad." Those are great places to start, but they simply scratch the surface of deep connection and understanding. To get greater effect when using emotional labels in communication, your goal as a listener is to respond with an analysis of emotions the person may not be saying directly. Sometimes they may not even realize what they are feeling. This would look almost like a paraphrase mixed with an emotional label, as in, "So, what I am hearing is that all you're going through is reminding you of the betrayal and embarrassment you have felt in the past."

Tony would later learn through study that this is tied to how the average brain characterizes words with emotional symbolism. When we speak to the average human being using emotional words, we are speaking to parts of their brain that respond quickly and with more neurotransmitter release than you'd see with other types of spoken words. He also learned that utilizing emotional labeling can actually 'pull' someone out of their amygdala and paralimbic region when they are in crisis. With an emotional label it has been shown in functional magnetic resonance imaging studies that you can get someone's brain excitement to shift from the amygdala to the right ventrolateral prefrontal cortex. Excitement of this area helps to diminish emotional reactivity in crisis situations. Tony learned that this didn't only work on the people that he communicated with, but even when he labeled his own emotions under stressful conditions.

Tony's Crisis Intervention training reinforced his belief that advanced communication skills could significantly enhance his ability to assist people during his calls, regardless of whether they were in crisis. Unbeknownst to Tony at the time, guiding the suicidal man through crisis communication had ignited a desire within him to pursue this aspect of his work further. Equipped with new tools and a deeper understanding of existing skills, Tony felt a heightened sense of enthusiasm to go out and make a positive impact. As the class concluded, students were exposed to realistic scenarios intentionally designed to induce stress in communicating with individuals in crisis. The program coordinators had enlisted individuals with personal experiences of mental health struggles or clinical involvement with clients facing mental health issues to authentically portray people in crisis, adding a valuable layer of realism to the training.

The students in the class were taking turns as they rotated through different scenarios; a suicidal person about to jump off a building, a person who was depressed and needing a crisis counselor, a tense traffic stop with an angry veteran, a person in crisis with family members adding fuel to the fire and finally the scenario that taught Tony a huge lesson. Tony walked into the room, not knowing what to expect. Students were to walk into this scenario in particular as if they had stopped to get a soda at a convenience store and a woman had run up to them with an empty stroller screaming, "She ran around the corner with my baby!" The woman would then point wildly to the corner of the building indicating where the subject had run off with her baby.

She looked insistently at Tony and his scenario partner, "Aren't you going to do something?!"

As Tony and his partner pied the corner of the building, he caught the view of the subject holding the baby. The baby, a doll in the scenario, was in the woman's right arm, clutched closely to her chest. The wild-eyed woman with her hair all over, had a knife in her left hand.

As soon as she caught a glimpse of the officers she screamed, "GET BACK!" and raised the knife. This was obviously not a shoot scenario given her agitated state, the amount of movement she was making and most importantly the baby in her arms.

Tony started, "Hey, I'm Antonio."

"GET BACK!" screamed the woman.

Tony tried again, "Hi, I'm Antonio, I am here to help."

The crazed woman yelled, "Help me?! You can help me by leaving me alone!"

Tony scanned his thoughts for his next comment. "Why do you have that baby?"

"Why do I have this baby? How dare you! This is MY baby!" screamed the woman as she brought the knife closer to her and the baby. Tony then really put his foot in his mouth.

"Calm down," he said as he raised his tone.

The woman reacted in kind and matched Tony's energy. Tony nervously looked to his partner who shrugged his shoulders and chuckled. The crisis situation degraded from that moment into a shouting match, and Tony never really recovered.

After 20 minutes, Tony heard the words, "End scenario."

The main instructor for the program, Derrick, looked at Tony and said, "So, we learned a lot from that," as he put a hand on Tony's shoulder. Tony felt embarrassed, but also knew he was here to learn so he prepared himself for the debrief.

Derrick started, "So, pretty good introduction man. I got the impression you were caught off guard by the seriousness of the scenario, but this could really happen. People with mental health issues, or in psychosis can be very unpredictable. Where do you think things started to degrade?"

Tony said, "Well, honestly, I felt my stress kick up when the mother was yelling at me to do something, and then I cleared the corner I saw the lady with the knife, and knowing myself I let that make me hyperfocus. I couldn't concentrate and think of ways I know how to communicate with people."

Derrick smiled kindly, "Yes, sir, that is kind of tricky. Our brain does that to us. When we are stressed, we can get a dump of the neurotransmitter cortisol in the brain. When that happens our ability to think clearly is negatively affected. Cortisol specifically interrupts certain pathways associated with memory, which makes it hard for us to access information that we know is somewhere in there. We can clear some of the blockage by taking some deep breaths and focusing on some simple questions to ask out the gate."

Tony nodded in agreement and then added, "Well, I screwed up a couple things. I told her to "calm down", which I know better than to do, but here we are. And I also went into 'ask, tell, make' mode."

Derrick then said, "Yeah, it can be difficult to stay out of that mode given we are trained to be the 'command presence' when we arrive. Some people have a hard time communicating because they can't put this attitude aside, but rest assured that your uniform, badge, taser and gun are already speaking the message of authority to the person just by you being there.

Communicating with them in a calm demeanor sends them a message your uniform and equipment can't. Another thing to be mindful of is matching someone's energy. People tend to not appreciate that, and for people in crisis it can just be a trigger for the person to go into a defensive or attack mode. We are trying to avoid that, so be the calm, reasonable one, and maybe the person in crisis will start to match your energy instead."

Derrick then turned towards the whole class. "Listen guys and gals, I can teach you every trick in the book to actively listen and you might use them to some success. However, if you don't learn to empathize from a genuine place, all the tricks in the world will fail in the most difficult crisis moments."

A female deputy from a neighboring Sheriff's department raised her hand and asked, "Sir, how do we apply this empathy correctly?"

Derrick then shared, "Well, let me define it in a relatable way first. Do you all have kiddos? Just picture getting out of the car at a grocery store, and you have your little girl. As you are rushing to get her out of the car, you go to close the car door and watch as that door, almost as if in slow motion, closes on your little one's thumb."

As Derrick planted the image, you could see across the faces of almost everyone in the group, the same look of sucking their teeth in pain or wincing. He then continued," That feeling right there, is pure empathy. You all felt that pain for your little one because we all know what it feels like to crush a finger in a door or hit it with a hammer. You have to find a way to feel that deeply when it comes to the pain, suffering or panic of the person you are communicating with. That is how you tap into it, and by default show the person you won't give up on them."

Tony was amazed at that description and the power that Derrick had just described. He knew he had to learn how to use this power to help people.

Derrick shook Tony's hand before the scenario training was over and all the students walked back into the main auditorium. As the training wrapped up, Tony learned that Derrick and some others in the room were members of a specially trained team called the Crisis Intervention Squad. The squad was dedicated to the response for crisis related calls and mental health transports for people that had been petitioned for danger to themselves or others. Tony loved the idea of doing that 40 hours a week. Learning that this existed as a detail made Tony see where he wanted to go with his career.

CHAPTER 10

INTO THE CHAOS

Following the Crisis Intervention Training, Tony returned to his regular duties on the street. Whenever he encountered mental health-related calls for service, he began incorporating the new skills he had acquired during the week-long training. Initially, it felt a bit awkward to integrate these new tactics, but he soon discovered that they complemented the communication skills he already possessed. With practice, Tony noticed that the use of these skills became more natural and seamlessly integrated into his interactions.

By this time, Tony had four years in the department and was very comfortable in his own skin. He had made good friends and connections and at that point had made it to a squad that specialized in neighborhood-level issues. The mission of the squad very much followed 'broken window' theory, and they would work as a team to address small issues in the neighborhoods to avoid it becoming a higher crime area. Early, low level intervention and enforcement on crime has been shown to have positive effects on larger scale crime. Nuisance issues, reports of drug houses and homeless encampments were Tony's new specialty.

Tony's beat area was busy, but he and his partner handled business well and he liked working with the community members. Tony found that using communication skills from the Crisis Intervention Training was even helping him in talking to community members about their complaints. He found that giving people genuine attention and then crafting his answers to them based on their perspectives gave people the opportunity to vent and then understand what the police response was going to be. Even in situations where Tony had to tell citizens that there wasn't anything the police department could do, he found that if he listened and expressed real understanding of their frustration's they would be more likely to come off the phone feeling better. Tony found another aspect of his position enjoyable – regular opportunities for public speaking. He derived satisfaction from these speaking engagements, as they provided a welcome change from the routine of dealing with homeless individuals on a daily basis.

One morning, after finishing the squad pre-shift workout, Tony sat down at his desk with his piping hot coffee and started going through his work emails. Many of the community members would send complaints via email, letting Tony and his partner know about issues in their area that they wanted to look into. As he was making his way through the emails, he noticed one that had to do with becoming a Collateral Duty Negotiator for the S.W.A.T. team.

This got Tony's attention immediately. Tony opened the email to find that there would be a testing process the next month for the position, and there were several openings. The details explained that successful applicants would be invited to a 40-hour F.B.I. negotiations training, then be certified as members of the department's negotiation team, and subject to call-out for critical incidents. Tony knew what he had to do; he sent an email reply to the negotiations coordinator expressing his interest and requesting a time to meet.

Tony entered the command station where the S.W.A.T. team was based, feeling somewhat out of place as a patrol officer. The tactical officers exuded intense energy and athleticism, giving Tony a few questioning looks in his uniform. Remaining respectful, he greeted each one he passed and apologized when he interrupted a couple of operators to inquire about Horus Brown's whereabouts. They pointed him towards some cubicles. Horus, a highly respected S.W.A.T. operator and negotiator, had spent 25 years in the department, with 15 of those dedicated to the S.W.A.T. team. Known for his commitment to negotiations, Horus was working on building a dedicated collateral team to allow operators to focus on tactical aspects while negotiators handled communication equipment and tactics.

As Tony came around the corner of the cubicle, there sat Horus at his computer. Horus quickly turned around to introduce himself, "Oh, hello, I'm Horus Brown." Horus was about 5'10", average build, with a flat top, eyeglasses, a mustache and had a very 'dad' demeanor about him. As they began to chat, Horus leaned back in his chair as he sat, put his arms behind his head and spread out like he was on a pool lounger, which Tony found a little comical. Horus shared the history of negotiations for the department and how he had become involved. Tony could sense an immense amount of pride and dedication relative to negotiations from Horus and it was obvious this was his passion. As Tony focused on asking his 'what's' and 'how's', Horus shared his vision for the program and what a potential new negotiator should be focused on.

As the conversation continued, Tony did his best to paraphrase what he understood Horus was looking for in a negotiator, what his next steps should be, and what the vision for the program was. Horus said, "Sounds like you got it."

He then added that the best candidate would be a team-player, have some basic knowledge and ability to apply communication skills, and possess a willingness to learn and be mentored. Tony did his best to show that he was willing to do what it took to make the team. All-in-all, the conversation was helpful. Horus gave Tony some paperwork to read through and a book recommendation. He then suggested that Tony reach out to the tactical Sergeants and the Lieutenant over the division. Tony arranged those meetings in the coming week, and he ordered the book. Tony had to chuckle to himself because when he received the book in the mail a few days later, there was a picture of Horus Brown on the cover. To be fair, it was not Horus's book, but it was a retired colleague of his who wrote the book and had Horus's image put on the cover.

As Tony delved into the book, he found himself questioning why this information wasn't universally presented to all officers. However, upon reflection, he acknowledged that not all officers shared the same enthusiasm for communication, and new recruits were already overwhelmed with information. The book provided a comprehensive overview of the history of tactical negotiations, originating in New York with the N.Y.P.D. and later developed by the F.B.I. The content covered team dynamics, positions and responsibilities, threat assessments, and aspects of Active Listening (A.L.S.), a concept Tony was familiar with from his New Start days and more recently from C.I.T. certification. With about three weeks before the testing, Tony couldn't read the entire book, but he gained a solid understanding of the fundamentals for participating in a crisis negotiations team and how the team should function. When the testing arrived, Tony performed well, earning an invitation to attend his first monthly negotiations team training a week later.

As he walked into his first training he recognized Derrick, the C.I.T. program coordinator who he had met in his previous training. Derrick had also tested onto the team the same time as Tony. They shook hands and sat down next to each other as Horus started the training. In the training room, Tony observed around 10 other individuals who had gathered for the session. Horus conveyed his enthusiasm for inaugurating the collateral-duty program, emphasizing that this marked the beginning of numerous training courses for the new negotiators. He went on to explain that he had conceived the idea for the team and was essentially constructing it from the ground up. Previously, S.W.A.T. operators randomly assigned to negotiations often led to suboptimal outcomes. While some operators surprised themselves with their negotiating skills, the reality was that those who drew the negotiations 'short straw' were typically discontented or distracted, longing to engage in tactical operations.

Horus outlined this new approach to create a dedicated group of communicators who were genuinely interested in the role. He expressed his commitment to training and leading everyone in the room to become proficient collateral negotiators, emphasizing the mandatory on-call standby days and readiness for callouts to critical incidents requiring advanced communication skills. Horus's excitement about the program was palpable, and it resonated with many in the room who were eager to be part of this innovative initiative.

In the subsequent month, Tony, Derrick, and the others participated in their 40-hour F.B.I. negotiations school. Interestingly, despite the presence of some accomplished F.B.I. agents during introductions and certain modules, it was Horus who predominantly led the classes. Tony later recognized that Horus's extensive involvement made sense, considering that negotiators from larger agencies tended to gain more exposure and experience in high-stress, high-stakes negotiations. While the F.B.I. agents provided valuable knowledge, Horus brought numerous real-world examples, experiences, and practical lessons to the training.

The course left Tony with a significant insight: the importance of making a subtle adjustment in his introduction. In basic negotiator training, he discovered that introductions held immense significance, as "first impressions can carry or crush a negotiation," as emphasized by one of the instructors. Delving into the psychological aspect, the instructor highlighted studies indicating that people form judgments about trustworthiness within a mere 33 milliseconds of meeting someone. Tony found this revelation fascinating. The instructor also discussed confirmation bias, emphasizing how humans tend to seek information that aligns with their initial beliefs, reinforcing their perception of trustworthiness or other traits.

The significance of first impressions in negotiations is highlighted by the impact they can have on the ease or difficulty of the process, as discussed by the instructor. Introducing oneself plays a crucial role, and the instructor advised, "You should do your best to be calm but also endearing with your introduction. It should sound something like, 'Hi, I am Tim, and I'm here with the police outside. I am here to talk with you about coming out.'" This approach is light yet non-threatening, effectively conveying who you are, the purpose of your presence, and the desired outcome without issuing threats or directives, as shared by the F.B.I. instructor.

As Tony thought about that, he penned down some intro's on his steno pad and reviewed them in the mirror at home that night with a digital recorder running. Something just kept sticking on his introductions, a hitch of sorts as he played them back to himself. Then it came to Tony, he had to get rid of, "Hi, I am Antonio." There was something about the length of his name that was just not working for him, so that is when 'Tony' became the default for Antonio. It flowed better, was easier for the person on the other line to remember, and just seemed a tad more friendly. "Hi, I'm Tony and I am out here with the police. My job is to get you out of there safely."

A year had gone by since the selection process for collateral negotiations. Tony had found his passion in this realm and dove in deeper than he ever had into anything before. When he worked, he used his skills constantly and never stopped pushing himself to improve. It wasn't that he believed he was better than anyone; actually to the contrary, he told himself that every call was an opportunity to improve himself, learn from mistakes and fine tune his craft.

When he wasn't working and testing his communication skills, Tony read books and articles about negotiations, then he re-read them and highlighted important points, making notes along the way, because he knew he didn't have a steel trap for a memory. He would listen to podcasts and interviews and voraciously search for the best advice he could about negotiations and influence. Tony had made friends along the way, and Derrick was one of them. Derrick had seen how hard Tony was working to learn the art and science of negotiation and was first to push for Tony to transfer over to the Crisis Intervention squad. Tony had wanted to work on that squad for a long time, and now it was an even better opportunity to practice powerful communication skills with people in crisis, people with cognitive issues and people with mental health issues. The challenge and opportunity were both things that Tony could not pass up.

After Tony was successful in the testing process for the Crisis Intervention position, he finished several weeks of riding with Derrick and a couple other members of the Crisis Intervention Squad to learn the ropes. It was then time for him to meet his new partner. That morning, Tony climbed into the unmarked white Tahoe, specially designed for mental health transports. Tony was elated to be on the squad. As he was loading up his equipment for the start of the day, in rolled his new partner. He had not met Monica yet. She had been finishing up the school year as a school resource officer when Tony came to the squad. After that she had been riding with another one of the officers on their detail and they hadn't crossed paths yet.

Monica stepped out of her personal vehicle, a bright smile beamed and a cheerful, "Good Morning," followed. The two shook hands and shared some typical introductory chit-chat. As they loaded up for the day, they both smiled and hoped for a safe one.

This first good day would blend into a thousand more over the years. The partnership was strong and Monica matched Tony's energy the vast majority of the time, and the two's strengths and weaknesses balanced each other on the street. Monica was a practicing counselor who was deeply empathic. These skills and her ability to converse genuinely would help Tony become a better Crisis Intervention officer as well as negotiator.

Tony had to laugh at the sense of humor the universe demonstrated when in their second week of partnership Monica turned to him and said, "I have to ask, I know you went to a university down south, but did you also work for the New Start program?"

The question took Tony by surprise because it seemed out of context. He hadn't thought about New Start for many years. He turned with a questioning look and replied, "Yeah, I was."

"I bring it up because I realized that you helped move me into my dorm at New Start!" said Monica.

"What? No way you could remember that."

Monica gave Tony a disapproving look, "First of all, I am a woman and a mom, so I have a super memory. Plus, I wasn't sure initially, but I checked this weekend and my dad had photos from that day and you are in them. You have the same goofy smile as you do now," said Monica.

"Wow, that is freaking insane," said Tony. They then trailed off into a conversation about their respective college experiences.

Later that night, and for years to come, Tony came to believe that there was something to the connection and the universe bringing the two back together. It was meant to be, and Tony was convinced that Monica was in his life to make him better.

*   *   *

"Beeeeeeeeeeeeep!" rang the hot tone over the channel Tony and Monica were monitoring as they drove through the city.

"Caller says that the ex-boyfriend broke into the home and raped her last night. She was just able to get out and he is still inside the apartment with a gun," said the 911 dispatcher over the radio. Tony's ear had perked up to the traffic being put out over the westside precinct channel.

He looked over at his partner Monica, "Let's slow roll that way, we aren't far."

She acknowledged and pulled up the call on their mobile data terminal. As he drove their Tahoe in the direction of the call, details continued to come in from 911.

"The caller is estranged from the ex-husband for about a year now. They have a child in common who the suspect has virtually no fatherly ties to. The suspect had showed up high on methamphetamines the night before and forced his way in through the front door while the victim was trying to convince him to go away. The victim is now with uniformed officers outside the apartment complex."

A catchy little ringtone jingled in Tony's pocket. It was Horus calling. Tony answered and Horus gruffly said, "You monitoring that traffic in the west precinct?"

"Yessir," said Tony in a joking tone.

Horus came back, "When you get there and assess, give me a heads up. The tactical Sergeant is listening." Tony confirmed he would do so and continued to the call address. As they pulled into the area, the apartment in question was surrounded and the suspect had noticed all the commotion.

The dispatcher cleared over the radio, "Suspect is calling 911 now and says that everyone needs to leave, or he is blowing his brains out."

Tony turned to Monica. "Wonder why they always word it like that."

Monica retorted, "Television and movies, plus it sounds super serious that way."

The patrol Sergeant asked over the radio if the Crisis Intervention Unit that had just pulled up could get on the phone with the suspect. In response, Monica cleared over the radio for dispatch to patch the suspect's 911 call to their cell phone. She then hopped out to get more intelligence from the patrol Sergeant Running the scene and asked Tony, "You got this?"

Tony replied, "Yeah, but when you get some intel come on back, I need a coach."

Just then Tony's work phone rang. Monica flashed him the peace sign and went to get more intel.

"This is Detective Mendoza," said Tony.

"Hi, this is Dispatch Supervisor Jenni. I have got the caller on the line for you, you ready?"

Tony told the dispatcher he was, and then he thanked her.

The next words over the line were, "Hey who the fuck is this?"

Tony started, "Hey man, this is Tony, and I am out here with the police. My job is to get you out of there safely."

"Nah, fuck that fool! I ain't coming out there, you putos are gonna' kill me," said the suspect.

"Fair enough," said Tony, knowing that the suspect wasn't just going to give up. Over time and with some experience Tony had learned that people in these types of situations need the ability to feel like they can say 'No' initially. It allows people a sense of autonomy and they aren't expecting to be treated with respect after saying 'No'.

Tony came back with, "So, what happened, how did we get to this point, man?"

As the compound question came off his lips, Tony kicked himself and thought, 'Dang it, Tony! One question at a time. Keep it simple and shut up!' So, Tony shut up and weathered a bit of awkward silence.

"Listen homes, I ain't comin' out. I've fucking been beat on by cops before, so fuck you and your little tricks!" The line went dead, and just as it did so Monica opened up the passenger car door. Tony cleared over the radio, "Command, we are off-line."

Officers at the scene then put out over the radio that they could see the suspect in the living room pacing, with the business end of a black semi-auto pistol in his mouth. Tony sensed his own anxiousness and remembered the power of labeling that emotion.

"I am feeling anxious," said Tony to himself quietly. He immediately felt relief from some of the pressure.

Monica asked, "You okay?"

Tony turned to her and nodded with a wink. Monica smiled and then said, "So, this guy is a piece of work. He has been in and out of her life for the last five years. He is a meth user and lives on the street pretty much chasing dope all of his days. The victim says he is super narcissistic and will play the 'poor me' card really well. She also said he has no interest in his son, so that will be a dead end. He loves meth and himself, not in that order."

"Well, that gives me a good place to start, thank you," said Tony. Then he added, "I'm getting back on-line with him now."

Tony dialed the number that dispatch had put in the call notes.

"Hey bro, stop calling or you're going to make me do something you'll regret!" yelled the suspect.

Tony, trying to mimic the suspect's speaking pattern a bit, replied, "Bro, I know this is a really bad situation and I also know I am bugging you but let me re-introduce myself. My name is Tony, what is your name?"

"Pssssshhhh, fuck that bro I ain't telling you shit," said the suspect.

Tony, remembering that this was another opportunity to reframe the situation, replied in a friendly tone, "No worries brother, we'll keep it casual. How you holding up in there?"

As Tony finished the question Monica rotated the in-car computer towards Tony to show him a picture of the suspect that she had pulled up. Above the photo it read, 'Martin Mendoza.' Martin looked like a Mexican Vin Diesel that had eaten too many tacos.

Monica wrote a playful note, "He is your cousin."

Tony frowned at her, shaking his head.

"Hey man, how the fuck you think I am holding up? My lady fucking kicked me out a while back and I got no place to stay now bro," said Martin, before adding, "I just wanted to see my kid last night and now she's trying to throw up some charges on me bro."

Tony empathized with Martin telling him how difficult that sounded, and how much he must sacrifice for his family, even though Tony knew this wasn't reality. Martin ate it all up like the tacos he apparently loved so much, and he was sure to tell Tony how hard he was trying to be a part of his kid's life. The irony of that was displayed when Monica showed Tony an outstanding child support warrant Martin had out for him for $10,000 in back child support. Tony, knowing this was all a narcissistic ploy by Martin, played along. Tony continued to put himself in Martin's shoes and try to see things through Martin's version of reality.

About an hour into the negotiation Martin gave the first sign that the tide of the conversation was changing by asking, "So, what kind of charges am I looking at here?"

This was a good sign. It indicated that Martin was not only thinking about the future, but that he was processing the consequences in a more rational manner. Tony had learned that it was better to be up front than to dance around the answer to that question.

"Look Martin, it looks like she is alleging you sexually assaulted her," started Tony.

Just then Martin interrupted, "What the fuck man!? Nah, see that's that bullshit right there. She was down for whatever last night, and now she wants to turn that shit on me!"

Tony paused quietly for a second then replied, "Martin, we agreed to be honest with each other and I am being honest with you. I am not going to lie. That being said brother, which is what she is alleging, but the detectives have to get your side of the story too."

"Damn bro, this is some shit," said Martin as he stifled some crying that may or may not have been real.

Tony added, "And you're a sharp guy, you know how it is man. That domestic violence stuff isn't something we walk away from. We have to investigate this completely, but you having a gun and not coming outside is making it hard to get things moving forward so people can hear your side. Plus, to be honest man, I have been on the line with you for a while, I am with you now and don't want to see you hurt yourself or get hurt."

Tony knew that throwing in some mention of unity paired with the prompting that he wasn't giving up on Martin might buy some positive rapport. The seeds had to be planted for Martin to envision cooperation and peaceful resolution.

"You're just like her bro, you know all the right shit to say huh, fucker?"

Tony reflected on his communication, realizing that he might have provided too much information. Understanding that excessive explanations can negatively impact rapport in a negotiation, he acknowledged the mistake. Instead of reacting emotionally or continuing to talk nervously, Tony wisely chose to pause and recalibrate.

Martin then filled the silence, "Hey fool, I'm fucking talking to you."

Tony took a quiet breath and calmly replied, "I know brother, but you seemed like you were really frustrated and needed to get that frustration out to me, I didn't want to interrupt."

"Yeah man! I'm frustrated as hell bro. I don't want to go to jail, and you fucking know I don't want to kill myself today!" Martin yelled. This was the second indication that the tide was changing.

Tony capitalized, "That is good to hear Martin. I don't want to see you hurt, so this is what happens next..."

As Tony finished describing the exit plan, Martin asked for a few minutes to clear his head and hung up the phone. Tony gave him two minutes and called back.

"What man!? I am trying to think, stop rushing me," snapped Martin.

"Martin, I told you my focus is your safety. Us staying in communication is the safest thing we can do," said Tony.

As the conversation continued Martin did some of the same last-minute stalling that Tony had seen before, needing to use the bathroom, wanting to finish their drink and of course the ten-minute shoe and sock routine.

Eventually Martin gave a heavy sigh and said, "Fine man, I'm coming to the door."

A few seconds later Martin was in custody and everyone on scene could breathe a little better. Tony walked up to the police Tahoe where Martin had been seated in cuffs.

"Hey man, I'm Tony. Nice to meet you in person."

Martin looked up, "Sup, you're that fool I was talking to huh? You did good man, thanks for having my back."

"You're welcome," said Tony, "I told you I always keep my word."

Reflecting on the negotiation that evening, Tony assessed his strengths and acknowledged moments when he almost got emotionally involved. While recognizing the need to avoid such pitfalls, he also admitted his weaknesses. Martin's astuteness in identifying Tony's influence tactics prompted self-reflection. Tony questioned if he had overly focused on tactics rather than being naturally present in the moment. Understanding the importance of genuine empathy, he recognized the distinction between using empathy as a tool and embodying it authentically. This realization fueled Tony's commitment to continual improvement in future negotiations.

CHAPTER 11

WHAT LOSS FEELS LIKE

As Tony worked to improve his communication skills, he delved intensely into reading about all kinds of negotiations, from sales, to procurement, to interpersonal, and legal negotiations. Tony's old friend and recruiter Larry had kept in touch with him over the years, and he loved the path Tony had taken. Larry had retired from the department and moved on to the business world where he was thriving and seemed very happy.

Periodically, Larry would send Tony a book or suggest other books about negotiations and social influence. He never missed an opportunity to tell Tony he was his biggest fan. Tony always felt humbled and grateful for Larry's friendship. While researching police negotiation material, Tony discovered valuable information in various areas. Despite the painstaking process, he found nuggets of useful knowledge. One significant lesson Tony learned from his readings emphasized the importance of setting aside personal needs during the negotiation process.

As Tony dug into this idea, he realized he had been approaching his negotiations with too much need. Tony had to be honest with himself and admit this need was fueled by his own ego. As Tony looked back at some of the critical calls he had been involved with the last couple years, he remembered feeling a type of anxiety going into some of the situations or even sometimes mid-negotiation anxiety. In analyzing this feeling, he saw that during those negotiations he often felt a need to bring a positive resolution through his abilities. The problem with that was in the realization that Tony had to be candid with himself and see that sometimes, no matter how good you are at negotiating or how hard you try, ultimately the person on the other end of the negotiation gets a vote in how that situation plays out.

"If we focus on the 'win' as our mission, we set ourselves up to fail, and worse yet, set ourselves up to potentially feel anxiousness in the communication, which can negatively affect our thought process, tone and tactics," Horus told Tony when they discussed the point one afternoon in Horus's office. Horus then added, "You also have to remember that the whole idea of win-lose is horrible framing anyway. There are times you can do everything right and it still doesn't go our way. That doesn't mean the process wasn't correct, it just means the variable of the person in crisis was not open to change."

Tony asked, "So, then how do you fight this thing, this need?"

Horus chuckled, "Well, the reality is that it is a decision, and it isn't easy. We all struggle to put the need aside, but a good start is to trust the process. A part of that is looking at the interaction differently, reframing it."

Tony nodded and said, "So, keeping in mind that every negotiation is a new, fresh interaction, and focusing on the process is a good start."

Horus nodded and said, "Yeah, think about saying, 'I need to have this car.'"

He gave Tony a serious look, "Close your eyes and let me hear you say it out loud."

Tony replied, "I need to have this car."

"Keep your eyes closed, and now say, 'I want to buy this car,' instead," directed Horus.

"What did you feel?"

Tony did so and opened his eyes. "That does feel different, wow."

"I don't know the exact process, but it does something in the mind, and changes the way you're thinking and even feeling about the situation," said Horus.

"That is pretty freaking cool," said Tony. "So, that is a start, but what else do I 'want' to do to reframe the scenario?"

Horus went on to explain to Tony that ego is another kryptonite for negotiators. He also described the great importance of knowing your mission, having a mission statement on paper and even having a personal mission statement.

"If you have your mission clear in your mind, and accessible at all times, you can always ask yourself if the action you are about to take in the negotiation serves the mission or hinders the mission. It helps keep you from allowing your ego to derail your work," shared Horus.

Horus then continued about the battle against ego and Tony was appreciative of the perspective that Horus's many years had brought him. Horus suggested that Tony go home that night and play with some different ideas for his own mission statement as a negotiator.

"Keep it simple, and remember it isn't about you, it is about the people you serve."

Tony now had his boy Enzo from his previous marriage, who was ten-years-old, and his three-year-old daughter Olivia, who he had conceived with his long-time girlfriend. After putting Enzo and Olivia to bed for the night Tony sat down at the kitchen table and started to jot down some ideas of his personal mission as a crisis negotiator. He remembered that Horus told him that the mission needed to be simple, easy to remember and be focused on service, not on yourself. As Tony racked his brain that night, looking through his highlighted books and notes from classes he had taken for the right wording, he fell asleep at the table, and woke up around 0100 to shuffle off to bed. Somehow Olivia had managed to take up all available space in the bed and Tony felt bad moving her so Tony ended up in the guest room for the night.

When he woke up that morning, Tony made himself an earl gray tea with some milk and sweetener. Tony had opted to switch to tea years back because it was less acidic. As he sipped his hot tea Tony sat back down at the table where his notes and books were spread out. He had apparently gotten off task the night before, because he couldn't figure out the train of thought he had put on paper as he was dozing. As he pieced the notes together, he realized he kept making the mistake of getting too detailed with the statement. This would make the mission statement hard to remember. Tony worked for a bit in the quiet of the morning and just as Olivia ran up to hug him from behind, he finished writing. Tony was then whisked off to make some breakfast for his little one and Enzo.

The following week, Tony presented his mission statement to Horus at the command station. Horus carefully read it a couple of times, as if processing the information, and then read it aloud, "*To provide patrol and the S.W.A.T. team the highest form of verbal and psychological de-escalation, while affording all subjects we are tasked to communicate with the opportunity for a violence free conclusion to the calls we respond to.*" He pondered for a moment and followed, "I like it."

Tony, knowing how picky Horus could be, said, "Really? That is great."

"Yeah, you kept it simple, and you put your ego aside," said Horus. "I also like how you focused on the fact that we do our best to present and communicate options to suspects for peaceful resolutions. Pretty good man," said Horus. As the afternoon came to an end, the two talked more about some of the calls they had recently been on together and eventually both men headed home for the day.

A few weeks later, Tony woke around 0500 to a call from Horus. Olivia was sleeping next to him, so he carefully rolled out of bed, so as to avoid disturbing her too much. Tony stepped out of the bedroom and into the guest room. When he looked at the phone, he saw he had missed a text message just two minutes prior for a callout. He always tried to sleep light knowing he was on standby, but apparently today it wasn't light enough. Tony answered, and Horus greeted him, "Good morning early riser, we have a callout."

Tony groggily questioned, "What we got?"

"Looks like it's a guy who is acting really paranoid, holding himself hostage with a knife inside of someone's shed up on the north side of town. Patrol apparently hit the guy with pepperball, and bean bag rounds to no effect and even tried tasing him without effect," said Horus in an exasperated tone.

From previous experience, Tony hated it when this happened because it would make building rapport with the person even more difficult, given force had already been used, but he knew he hadn't been at the original scene and didn't know all the details patrol was dealing with.

"Okay man, I'll check the text thread for the address and radio channel, see you out there."

Tony got dressed quickly and as he was doing so he sent a text message to his tia so she could come keep an eyes on the kids. As soon as his tia got to the house Tony rushed out as quietly as he could. As he responded, he turned on his radio to hear the updates. He could hear that patrol had established a perimeter around the backyard, where a small metal shed was located. They were waiting on a negotiator to arrive since the subject seemed to be delusional and was not responding well to any of the patrol officers on the scene, despite attempts to use force to control him.

The owners of the house had been evacuated according to the supervisor on scene and wanted prosecution for the trespassing. As Tony arrived, he could see the bright orange car parked in an odd position next to the backyard of the home that was surrounded by patrol officers. Tony walked up to the Sergeant on scene and asked what the story was. Apparently, the subject had originally been in the car with his girlfriend when they parked there around 0300. The male subject had started to scare her with his paranoid behavior and the girlfriend just wanted to leave. She eventually escaped the vehicle and called 911 because she didn't know what else to do.

After his girlfriend had exited the vehicle, he had apparently been scared and jumped the wall into the home next to where he had parked. The subject then proceeded to hide in a small metal shed in the backyard. According to the girlfriend, he had been having an episode of bipolar mania and was using cocaine as well the night before. She also shared that he had recently been very paranoid and believed that someone was trying to kill him and her, when he pulled over in the dirt lot earlier that morning.

Tony saw the name written on the card, "Marcos Garcia." Then it clicked. Tony recalled that he had been assigned to talk to Marcos before. It happened in the middle of a November day, just before he and Monica were about to take their lunch break. Marcos had been extremely paranoid and on drugs several months back when he climbed on his family's roof and proceeded to throw off almost all the tile shingles down at officers who had arrived in reference to a call of a man on a roof.

Tony, Monica, Derrick and the rest of the Crisis Intervention Squad had spent two hours trying to get Marcos down that day. It was definitely a parallel approach because Marcos was not responding much to Tony while on the roof, and he had little response to even the less-lethal munitions used on him by the S.W.A.T. team. Eventually Marcos responded to a third-party recording (T.P.R.) from his mother that the team played over the public announcement system in a patrol Tahoe, and was convinced enough to come to the ladder that they had placed for him on the roof. Once there, he stalled for quite some time and was eventually convinced by another few less-lethal rounds to come down the ladder. Marcos was taken into custody that day and charged with aggravated assault for attempting to hit the patrol officers with the roof tiles.

Fast forward to that early morning in the backyard, and Marcos was not acting much different than how he had acted on his family's roof. Marcos had threatened officers with his knife defensively, but he had never left the shed to lunge at them. Apparently, he had been pepperballed when he came out of the shed for a moment. Marcos had been showing a bit of compliance to commands, but was pepperballed and hit with bean bag rounds when he didn't do what the officers wanted him to fast enough.

Tony grabbed his jaw, and dragged his palm down towards his chin when he heard this. He shook it off though because it didn't matter. All that mattered was that Marcos needed help seeing what was safest today for him.

Tony started in English, "Marcos, I don't know if you'd remember me, but I remember you cause we worked together before. My name is Tony, and I am here to help you come out of there safely."

Marcos was moving around the shed, knife in his left hand, and didn't appear to be paying attention. Tony reintroduced himself again, and Marcos still gave no response. It sounded as if Marcos was talking to himself inside the shed and through the partially open shed door Tony could see some movement. Tony then moved into some non-responder dialogue. As he was about 20 minutes into the non-responder protocol, S.W.A.T. officers had started to show up. As their movements to take over perimeter positions were being shadowed by the rising sun, Marcos was clearly agitated.

Tony considered that all the movement was probably making Marcos nervous. When he shared his thoughts over the radio, Derrick walked up behind him and put a hand on his right shoulder, quietly saying, "Behind you buddy, what do you need?"

Tony felt a sense of relief to have a team member with him. He gave Derrick a quick rundown of Marcos's erratic behavior in the shed and reminded Derrick that they had talked to this young man before.

Derrick remembered and said, "Oh yeah, he was a tough one man."

Tony looked back at Derrick and replied sarcastically, "Thanks buddy, no pressure," then winked at Derrick.

Derrick then reminded Tony he had done some of his communication in Spanish the last time he communicated with Marcos and that seemed to have some effect when he was on the roof.

"Marcos, estoy aquí para ayudarte a salir de el cobertizo, mientras mantienes tu seguridad," started Tony. Marcos lowered the knife a bit, turned towards Tony and for the first time that morning he acknowledged Tony. Tony kept his communication in Spanish from that point on. He and the team later learned that Marcos's father, who spoke primarily Spanish, was very influential to Marcos.

As the negotiation continued, about two hours in, Marcos was extremely close to dropping the knife out of the shed door at one point, but something spooked him as he was about to do so. It was difficult to tell what had startled him because Marcos was clearly battling internal stimuli the whole time. At this point, it appeared that Marcos's psychosis had gotten the better of him. Tony and Derrick could tell that this was a negative turning point but maintained their poise and continued forward. Derrick kept coaching Tony, and they continued with the dialogue in Spanish. As time passed, Tony was asked by the tactical sergeant to change the tone a bit and let Marcos know there would be unfortunate consequences if he continued to refuse compliance. They had also learned from the negotiator assigned to work intelligence that in addition to the trespassing today, Marcos had a valid felony warrant for not appearing in reference to the charges from the instance where he was throwing tile at the officers on the previous incident.

Tony switched the dialogue a bit, trying to still maintain a calm tone, while communicating a serious message. Tony tried in English to switch it up. "Marcos, right now we have an opportunity, and I don't want you to lose this opportunity for us to work together to a peaceful conclusion here." He then repeated the same message in Spanish. Neither seemed to have any effect, but Tony kept at it.

Tony was doing his best to employ empathy and understanding in his words and tone, although Marcos had never been any more responsive than a couple of inaudible statements and intense looks. It was a challenging negotiation and as Tony tried hard to feel what Marcos might be feeling, he could sense that Marcos must be feeling terror in the tiny space. Soon the tactical Sergeant elected to move Tony and Derrick into the armored vehicle that had arrived on scene.

As Derrick and Tony hopped in the armored vehicle they said 'hey' to their buddy Bobby, the senior officer on the Specialty Vehicles Detail. Bobby was a top-notch driver and an all-around nice guy. They shared their typical quick greeting for an event like this and Bobby handed Tony the microphone for the public announcement system. Bobby then pulled the armored vehicle up to the wall the shed was adjacent to, tapping the block wall with the heavy bumper. Tony could see through the crack in the door that Marcos quickly reacted and was jumping up and down in the shed.

One of the S.W.A.T. operators cleared over the radio that Marcos was motioning wildly inside the shed. Tony tried to use the break in communication and introduction of the armor to gain Marcos's attention anew.

"Marcos, as you can see, just as I had tried to tell you, things are getting more serious here. Consider what I told you before, we still have a little time to work together here," said Tony. All Tony could see was the shed shaking as Marcos hit the walls with his fists. This movement concerned the tactical team, and preparation began to address that.

A short time later Tony heard, "Gas deployed," over the radio and two 'thunk' sounds from the direction of the main house. A grayish smoke started to build up inside the shed and slowly began to come out of the shed door and seems where the body of the shed met the roof. Marcos could be seen moving around violently and Bobby got on the radio to let the tactical officers know what he was seeing from his vantage point in the armor. Soon the cloud of gas took effect and out jumped Marcos. Marcos leapt on the top of the shed with what appeared to be the knife in hand. He was quickly confronted and engaged by the S.W.A.T. operators, but Marcos was not complying. It was hard to tell whether Marcos still had the knife because of the limited visibility created by the gas emanating from the interior of the shed. Tony then heard two more 'thunks' and "less-lethal deployed," followed over the radio. Marcos then jumped from the shed roof onto the of the masonry block wall toward the armor, but then back to the roof of the shed. Two more rounds of less lethal were deployed at Marcos and he turned to run from the top of the shed, but fell off. As Marcos fell, Derrick, Tony and Bobby lost sight of him in the smoke of the gas.

The tactical officers moved slowly up to Marcos's position and cleared over the radio that he was not moving. One of the operators advised that Marcos had dropped the knife when he fell, and they had kicked it to the side. Another of the operators then advised they had Marcos detained but needed the fire department to respond immediately. As Tony, Derrick and Bobby looked out of the armored vehicle, they watched the tactical officers carefully carrying Marcos back towards a clear area where fire department staff could check his vitals.

Tony's heart sank. Marcos lay there, with a clearly broken arm, bleeding heavily from his face and he was not moving. The fire department worked feverishly to check his vitals and place him on a backboard. As the scene continued to unfold, time felt like it stopped for Tony. An ambulance eventually arrived, and they placed Marcos on a gurney to be transported. As the sirens of the ambulance kicked on, all Tony could do was hope Marcos was okay and wonder what he could have done better to help.

In the days following the event, Tony felt burdened, as if a cold, heavy vest pressed down on his shoulders and chest. His head throbbed, not quite like a headache, but akin to a mild hangover. The dull, cloudy ache persisted. Tony became noticeably quieter in the car with Monica and at home. One night, as he tried to relax, he unexpectedly teared up at a slightly emotional scene on television. Surprised, he wiped his eyes, chuckled, and muttered to himself, "What's wrong with me?"

The next day as Monica, Derrick and Tony sat having lunch together Tony blurted out, "I think I am messed up, guys." Both Derrick and Monica looked inquisitively at Tony. "I think that call last week jacked me up. I don't know if it was because I was negotiating in Spanish and he got hurt, or maybe because of how hurt I saw that dude get right in front of me, but something isn't right."

Monica, who was also a practicing clinical mental health therapist was the first to respond. "No, you're a human being, who cares deeply about what you do, and you tried your hardest to help that guy. It pierced you deeply when you saw him hurt after investing so much emotion and energy into the communication that morning."

"I guess, I am just really confused and feel like I took a big hit," shared Tony.

Derrick then started, "I think we have talked about this before man, but this call is just a lot more real and in your face. It is a tough one, but we can't help everyone. You know this. It is only a real loss if you didn't do everything to prepare for that moment. I know that is not the case for you or us as a team. We were ready and we all wanted to help that guy."

Monica then added, "It's okay for you to feel the hurt, that is what is going to happen if you get too deep into that empathy. It is a tough balance. Please just keep in mind that even though you may feel negatively about the incident, you didn't do anything wrong and neither did the team or the tactical guys. Try and remember other times you didn't get the outcome you had hoped for on one of these calls, but there were positive aspects about the resolution anyways. You know, like the times you got someone separated from a gun before S.W.A.T. confronted him, or when you got someone to come out of the house, even if there was minor damage done, but you avoided heavier consequences for that person and their property. If you can say you tried with every ounce of effort and empathy, then you did your best for that person and the community. Ultimately the people we are talking to always have a say in the outcome."

Tony felt better given the kind words from his friends and colleagues.

CHAPTER 12

THE UNEXPECTED

Monday morning had rolled in like the juggernaut it always is. Tony and Monica stopped at a coffee shop so that Tony could get an earl gray tea with a splash of milk, and Monica could get her plain, dry bagel. As they caught each other up about their respective weekends they cruised through town. Fall was bringing some relief from the sapping heat they had been dealing with all summer, so they could actually roll around without air conditioning running, and windows open.

As they were chatting away Tony heard a hot call go out about a stabbing on the west side, in the industrial district. Tony switched to that precinct's radio channel to listen to the traffic, being nosey.

"Caller is saying that her boss is down inside the office with the suspect who just stabbed the boss," voiced the dispatcher.

"Wow, that one sounds interesting," said Tony. Monica pulled the call up on their mobile data terminal. They started to roll that way.

Dispatch soon advised, "The female caller says that this is an employee who stabbed the manager. They believe that he is not well."

As officers started to advise that they arrived on scene Tony and Monica could hear that the officers sounded amped.

A female officer cleared over the radio, "Okay, the victim was able to crawl out of a back door of the warehouse offices. Suspect inside yelling out at us, brandishing a knife."

The Sergeant got on the radio and started issuing orders and assignments. Monica grabbed the radio and let the Sergeant know they were on their way to help with communications. Derrick, who wasn't too far behind Tony and Monica, added himself to the call.

As they arrived on scene, Tony parked their Tahoe down the road from the large industrial building lined with reflective windows. Tony could see officers scurrying into different positions and grabbing the tools needed for the perimeter. A fire truck was on scene and the paramedics were loading the victim onto a gurney. The man was covered in blood, and Tony could tell in the paramedic's face that there was a sense of urgency to get the man loaded. The ambulance doors closed and as it sped down the road, its lights and sirens blared. The ambulance was followed by a patrol Tahoe.

Walking up to the building, a stack of officers had piled up on both sides of the door to the office section of the building. The door had been propped open and appeared to lead down a long hallway. Tony could hear yelling inside and a Native American male popped his head out of a door down the hall. Because the view was obstructed Tony couldn't see what, if anything, the suspect was holding. The female officer who had cleared over the radio initially was a couple officers back in the stack of officers.

She called out to the suspect, "Hey dude, your life isn't over!" The man yelled something back that Tony couldn't make out.

"Dude, it is all going to be okay."

Tony cringed. As the man continued to yell, he popped out into the hallway and challenged the officers. An officer with a taser fired the less-lethal tool and missed, angering the suspect. He popped back into the office he had emerged from and yelled out, "See you fuckers aint shit!"

Tony and Monica looked at each other, and immediately walked over to the scene Lieutenant who was running things.

"Sir, we are here to help with communications, but we can't do that with the current setup. What are your thoughts on backing up from that front door if we can offer you some communications equipment?" asked Monica.

The Lieutenant knew Tony and Monica from previous barricades they had worked on together. He nodded slowly as if thinking, "Yeah, yeah, let's get these officers back and get your equipment lined up."

Monica thanked the Lieutenant. Tony and Monica set up the Norstan communication unit and it was ready to deploy in minutes. The Lieutenant had worked his magic and moved two police Tahoe's up to the front door to slow down any attempts of exit by the suspect and to create a barrier for the suspect in the case he attempted to assault officers. As that had moved into place, the female officer who had been talking to the suspect, continued attempts at communication. The suspect was talking back to her, but the officer was matching the suspect's energy too much, adding fuel to the fire.

Monica let the Lieutenant know they were ready with the equipment and his officers on scene took a shield, a rifle, and a couple more officers with them to escort Tony to deploy communications equipment. Tony tossed the communication box into the hallway as gingerly as possible. Tony then made his way back to this Tahoe, where he had set up their equipment on a table to the rear. As Tony had been deploying the box, he heard the female officer trying to calm the suspect down.

Tony stopped himself, put his ego aside and tapped the officer on the shoulder, interrupting her. "Hey, I am one of the negotiators, how would you like to come back and continue this from a safer position?"

The officer smiled and said, "Yes, please."

As Tony got the officer to their Tahoe, she introduced herself as Harley.

"Nice to meet you. You have been the voice this guy has been hearing, so I want to keep it consistent for him. I am going to coach you through this Harley. We are going to work some good stuff here, but the first thing we are going to do is stop calling him 'dude'," said Tony.

Harley nodded in agreement. Tony then explained the equipment, and how it operated. Harley seemed to get the gist of the equipment, although she looked very nervous.

"Now get on, re-introduce yourself, and pause," Tony directed. Harley followed the directions but tripped up for a second and stopped speaking.

"Take some deep breaths before you start back up, now I want you to explain how the box works," explained Tony.

Harley proceeded and about five minutes into her attempts, they could both hear voices through the communications equipment addressing the suspect, who Monica had now identified as Kendrick Yazzie. Tony gave Harley a confused look and took off his monitoring headset, "Who the hell is talking to the suspect?"

Monica looked surprised, and said she had no idea. Derrick had showed up around this time and told Tony, "I'll figure it out bud."

As Tony had Harley pause, Derrick went to make contact with S.W.A.T. operators closest to the open door. Apparently, Kendrick had started yelling at the operators when they took their positions, they had forgotten their discipline and started talking back. Derrick got the attention of the operators by the door as started, "Guys, we need you to stop talking to him."

When the operators saw Derrick, they immediately yelled to Kendrick, "This guy here is a negotiator and is going to talk to you." Derrick was frustrated but didn't want that to come across, so he started communicating with Kendrick.

"Hey sir, my name is Derrick, and I am with the police."

"Fuck you and fuck all these cops!" yelled Kendrick.

Derrick raised his voice, "Hey listen, I am here to help you, but I can't help you if you won't communicate."

At this point Tony was listening over the communications device. He was concerned because, as the communication progressed, Derrick appeared to be matching Kendrick's energy. Tony looked at Monica, and asked, "How do you feel about going up to coach Derrick?"

Monica made her way to Derrick's position. The tactical operators hadn't noticed that Derrick had put himself in an exposed position, in front of the police Tahoe. From experience, this was something that seemed to happen a lot in face-to-face negotiations. Tony, Monica, and Derrick were well aware of this 'creep up' effect and had discussed it multiple times, but even with awareness it would sometimes still make its appearance. Monica gently grasped the back of Derrick's outer vest and pulled

Derrick back behind the cover of the engine block and A-pillar of the Tahoe.

Derrick looked back, recognizing what Monica was doing and mouthed, "Thank you."

Derrick and Kendrick were still kind of shouting back and forth and Monica told Derrick, "Hey, slow down a bit and don't match what he is throwing at you." Derrick nodded affirmatively and took a deep breath.

Kendrick yelled, "What the fuck did that bitch just say to you? You guys are planning how to kill me. Guess what motherfucker?! I want to do that today, and I am gonna' make you assholes do it. ALL GOOD!" Just then Kendrick popped out of the office, holding a boxcutter in hand. He taunted the S.W.A.T. operators but didn't approach or threaten them. The operators showed incredible restraint and didn't react to Kendrick which appeared to frustrate him, and he jumped back into the office.

Derrick and Monica kept working the situation for another 10 minutes from the position by the open door, when the tactical Sergeant requested that the negotiators make their way back from the building. This was a result of Horus arriving on scene and speaking with the Sergeant, expressing that he didn't feel comfortable for Monica and Derrick's safety in their current position. There was also discussion about using explosives to breach the glass outside the office area, and the operators not being sure of how much broken glass would be projected out from the building if they did so. As Derrick and Monica made their way back to their unmarked Tahoe, Tony addressed Harley and explained that he was going to have Derrick keep working the communication from that point on. Harley seemed relieved and thanked Tony. Tony then handed Derrick the headset for the Norstan communication unit. Derrick apologized for jumping in and Tony let him know that he knew it was not Derrick's intent.

Tony smiled, handed Derrick the headset and said, "Let's get to work."

Derrick started back up, "Kendrick this Derrick, I took a step back from the building and I am speaking through this communications box now."

Derrick explained the unit again.

Kendrick yelled back," I don't give a shit how you talk to me I am still going to die today!" Tony had taken up the position of coach for Derrick.

He passed Derrick a note, "What makes you say that, Kendrick?"

The silence lasted about 20 seconds, but Derrick and Tony were both comfortable with it. Finally, the patience paid off, Kendrick began to yell, "Cause, I killed that mother fucker, and I am not going back to jail!"

Derrick pulled his headset to the side, "Is the boss dead?" he asked the team.

Monica overheard the question and told Tony, "I will go find out from the officer that escorted the ambulance."

Derrick calmly replied to Kendrick, explaining that the goal was a safe, peaceful resolution. This appeared to get Kendrick angrier, but Derrick didn't react. Kendrick began to hit one of the windows of the building and started yelling for the S.W.A.T. operators to kill him. Tony wondered if Kendrick was doing drugs in the office, because he was maintaining anger for a lot longer than the average person normally would. Shortly after Tony had that thought, Monica came back and let Tony know that she was still trying to find out about the condition of the victim but that she had found out from Kendrick's family that they believed he was Schizophrenic. This made more sense to Tony given Kendrick's altered mental state and level of energy. Tony shared the information with Derrick.

According to the family members that Monica spoke to on scene, Kendrick had been very distraught as of late and not sleeping. They showed up because Kendrick had called them and told them he had stabbed his boss. The family members let Monica know that Kendrick had recently been obsessing over the delusion that his boss was a pedophile and had been paranoid that there was a group of pedophiles trying to kill him, his boss being one of them. Kendrick had been staying up to all hours of the night and creating all kinds of stories in his mind.

Family members were extremely worried because Kendrick had called to apologize and say 'goodbye' to them that morning, but they didn't know what was going on. All they knew was that Kendrick had gone to work that morning. Horus and Monica jumped on that information and started looking into the boss, to see if there was any history of criminal behavior, or if there was anything that indicated the boss might be a child predator, or registered sex-offender. Monica could not find anything indicating that the victim had any ties to or allegations of sexual misconduct.

Monica next spoke with the administrative assistant, Judy, who had called 911. Judy was understandably upset and hadn't been able to stop crying since she had escaped the building. Monica was able to get her to calm down and focus long enough for her to give her statement. Judy shared that she had started her day looking through mail and separating it out for the bosses. She had heard a commotion in the manager's office just before she walked in to find Kendrick on top of the victim. Judy said

Kendrick had been behaving very oddly as of late, had been unfocused for weeks and showing up late every day.

Today was the day that their boss was letting Kendrick go. Just prior to the attack Kendrick had been called into the boss's office. Judy said that when she saw Kendrick on top of their boss, she instinctively grabbed the back of Kendrick's shirt. "When he turned around," she said, "he had a wild look in his eyes that I have never seen. He yelled at me and then raised a blood-covered boxcutter to threaten me, and I just ran."

Judy began to cry again, and Monica tried to console her. Shortly after Monica came back to share the information with Tony.

Derrick and Tony had been working diligently together to de-escalate Kendrick and as they did so, noticed that it was very hard to hear using the communication equipment they had deployed. Given the poor acoustics of the hallway where it had been deployed it seemed like they were catching more background noise than Kendrick's voice most of the time. They communicated this to Horus who started working on a solution. Kendrick's cell phone had died, according to him and would go straight to voicemail when Monica tried calling it. In the chaos of the moment Kendrick hadn't even considered charging the phone.

Horus brought this to Tony's attention and Derrick soon asked Kendrick, "Are you opposed to taking a moment to look for a charger for your phone?"

"Why the fuck would I do that?" asked Kendrick sarcastically.

Derrick explained, "I am just having a hard time hearing man. I have a damn hearing aid already and this communication equipment makes it hard for me to hear with the hearing aid." Tony gave Derrick a thumbs up.

Kendrick replied, "Ahhh shit man, I didn't know that, that's fucked up. Let me check."

This was the first sign of Kendrick showing some empathy, and Derrick could sense that showing that bit of weakness had gained him something with Kendrick. Derrick could hear Kendrick opening cabinets and drawers as if searching.

"Fuck yeah! Found one," said Kendrick.

Derrick then said, "That's great man, thank you, appreciate you for being willing to charge your phone." He then gently added, "What do you think about talking on the office line until we can get that puppy charged a little bit?"

Kendrick agreed, and within, 30 seconds Derrick found himself on the office landline with Kendrick. "So can you fucking hear now or what bro?"

Derrick smiled at Tony and replied, "Yeah man, much better, thanks." This was the first sign of improvement since they had started communication at the open door two hours before. Derrick and Tony continued to try chipping away at Kendrick's position, and he was not budging much. Derrick used the tactics of rationalizing the crime, minimizing the situation and even projecting fault for the circumstances on the victim. None of the tactics struck a chord with Kendrick. He seemed obsessed with his decision to have the police kill him and was very cyclical in his communication with Derrick.

At multiple points Kendrick would call out the positions of the S.W.A.T. operators outside the mirrored glass of the office he had tucked into. He would describe the operators in great detail and try to describe the tools they were holding.

Tony wrote Derrick a message, "Let's use the tools. Focus on how we have lots of ways to handle the situation that won't kill him."

Derrick read the note and said to Kendrick, "Kendrick, how do you see this playing out?"

"Shit bro, when I am ready, I am going to come at you guys, and you'll have to kill me. Simple as that."

Derrick paused, then came back, "Kendrick I hate to burst your bubble, but in this day and age, that isn't how things work. We have all kinds of tools we use to take someone into custody, even violent people, without killing them and all that you are risking is getting yourself hurt. Preserving your life is a priority to us."

This statement seemed to enrage Kendrick, and he began a tirade to the operators just outside the windows. As he banged on the glass, Sergeant Marsh cleared over the radio, "No one but the negotiator talks to him." The operators all maintained their discipline.

"Don't fucking ignore me!" yelled Kendrick.

Derrick's calm voice chimed in over the phone, "Kendrick, they aren't going to address you, I am the one that you are talking to."

"Fuck! Fuck! Fuck!" yelled Kendrick as he beat the desk in front of him and threw a computer to the ground. The phone line went dead.

Tony looked at Derrick and mouthed, "Are we off-line?"

Derrick confirmed the line was dead.

"Okay, I think this is as good a time for a break as any brother," said Tony and quickly opened up the window to let Horus know that they were off-line so he could put it out on the radio. "You are rocking it man. That guy doesn't trust anyone here but you."

Monica then opened the passenger side of the door, "Hey guys, you are doing awesome."

Derrick smiled. "So, what are your thoughts, Monica?" said Tony.

"Well, he is a tough nut to crack. He hasn't acted on the threats to use our officers to commit suicide yet, so I don't know that he will on his own. I think when they go in there, he might use that adrenaline rush as the catalyst to make them kill him," shared Monica.

Both Tony and Derrick were in agreement. "I think we just keep telling him that it isn't going to go the way he thinks, and he is going to get himself hurt before he is taken into custody," said Derrick.

Tony agreed, and also added that they had to keep pressing the idea that they weren't going to give up on Kendrick. At the four-minute mark they prepped to call back into the office. Monica began to shut the car door and then caught herself, "I almost forgot! The boss is not dead. Serious injuries to the abdomen and he will need plastic surgery to the face, but he is stable."

Both Tony and Derrick nodded in acknowledgement and Tony mouthed, "Thank you," with a thumbs up.

"What man?" answered Kendrick with an exasperated tone.

"Hey Kendrick, just wanted to give you a second to breathe since you seemed pretty upset," started Derrick.

"Yeah man, I am upset."

Derrick paused, "Kendrick I think I have some good news for you."

"What the fuck could be good news at this fucking moment?" Kendrick replied.

"Well, your boss isn't going to die. He is in stable condition."

"What the fuck man!? Goddamn it!" yelled Kendrick. Tony looked at Derrick, both confused by the reaction, but Tony wrote Kendrick a note, "stay silent." Derrick nodded. The silence grew thick on the line, as if pressure were building in Derrick's ears as if climbing in a plane.

Just then Kendrick broke the silence, "Damn, I didn't even do what I came here to do." Silence again.

Derrick was the one to break it this time. "I am sorry Kendrick, I am a little confused. What does that mean?"

"Like I said, I didn't come here to do what I came to do. I am a screw-up, even at this," uttered Kendrick.

Tony wrote to Derrick, "Not what we expected, but run with it." Derrick nodded in agreement.

"Well, this could be a good thing for you Kendrick," said Derrick. Kendrick shot back with an angry tirade, but there was a different tone in the anger, tired almost. As they continued the dialogue Derrick seemed to lose steam. He was no longer yelling at the operators outside the building, his energy was low, and his speech appeared labored.

Tony and Derrick grew concerned enough that they decided to ask, "Kendrick, did you do something to yourself in there?"

"Like what?" said Kendrick.

"Did you cut yourself?" said Derrick.

"Nah bro, I don't get down like that, you guys are going to have to do that," mumbled Kendrick, but there was no longer any conviction in his voice. Monica had heard the exchange and shared Kendrick's status with Horus, who passed the information along to Sergeant Marsh.

As Derrick tried to re-open the topic of Kendrick coming out peacefully, Kendrick stalled and asked to use the restroom. Derrick told Kendrick that them staying on the line together was the best thing for Kendrick's safety. Kendrick didn't disagree. Derrick stayed silent on the line, and Kendrick made a joke, "Hey bro, you're gonna' have to sing or some shit so I can go. Make a running water sound."

Derrick chuckled. "You don't want to hear me sing a damn thing man, it might ruin you."

At that moment there was a commotion on the line. Derrick and Tony wondered if Kendrick had fallen or had passed out. "Kendrick, Kendrick, are you okay?" No answer. "Kendrick, I have to know if you're okay or if you need an ambulance, call out to me or to the officers by the door," implored Derrick. Silence.

Tony hollered out the car window to Horus, "Something is up, he isn't answering anymore, and it sounds like he fell or something."

Just then a panicked Kendrick came across the line, "Hey Derrick! Derrick you there?"

Derrick replied, "I am here bud, you okay?"

"Yeah man, you won't fucking believe it, but I had been talking to you with my airpods in and it fell out and into the toilet," said Kendrick, "I thought I had lost you."

Derrick assured him that all was okay and made sure to ask if Kendrick was okay. The team all agreed, this was a good sign that Kendrick was in a different place emotionally and psychologically. About this time things changed tactically. Horus had been communicating the change in demeanor with tactical and Sgt. Marsh had discussed the matter with the tactical Lieutenant. Taking the updated information into account they asked Horus and the negotiations team to pressure the suspect more. Tony shared the request to Derrick and he started to discuss the consequences of Kendrick losing the opportunity to work with Derrick anymore. Kendrick told Derrick he didn't like this at all, but expressed he didn't want to stop talking with him. Kendrick started to play the stall game.

The negotiation had gone on for four hours and the tactical Lieutenant expressed that they had given the suspect ample opportunity to make some safer decisions. There had been discussion of taking a 'cannon-for-the-fly' approach, in which the armored vehicle's battering ram would be fitted with an end that was capable of penetrating one of the glass windows and introducing an immense amount of gas into the room Kendrick had been inside.

This was eventually set aside as a secondary option, given the potential amount of damage to the building this tactic would result in. As the tactical discussions continued, Derrick and Tony kept working on Kendrick. Kendrick's energy level remained low, but he claimed he was fine. Tony was soon advised that tactical would be sending in some gas from a 40-millimeter launcher, which he shared with Derrick.

"THUMP!" was followed by a, "CRASH!" in Derrick and Tony's ears, and Kendrick threw the box cutter with dried blood to the ground. As tactical operators announced that Kendrick was separated from his weapon, they closed in and took him into custody. Kendrick never put up a fight.

Derrick and Tony made their way over to where Kendrick had been placed in the back of a patrol car. The fire department was making their way over, but before they contacted Kendrick for treatment, Derrick introduced himself. Kendrick was covered in sweat, his eyes closed and nose running from the gas he had been exposed to. He grunted back to Derrick.

Derrick asked him, "What kept you inside of there man?"

Kendrick mumbled back, "I can't believe I couldn't even kill that chomo."

Derrick asked, "What do you mean?"

"Bro, I came to kill that bastard and keep the world safe from him, and I couldn't even do that right. Nothing mattered after that point man. I failed." Kendrick then put his head down, and the fire department began to check his vitals.

As Tony and Derrick walked away, Tony asked, "You good man?"

Derrick stayed quiet for a moment, and then replied, "Yeah man, I feel good. We did a really good job, and that dude didn't get hurt."

Tony smiled and nodded in agreement, "You just kept on with the genuine message that you were there for him, and you weren't going to give up on his safety. That carried the day brother."

As they continued their walk back to the Tahoe Derrick followed with, "It is weird how we really took the wind out of his sails with the fact he didn't actually kill the guy. People usually find that a relief."

Derrick had a perplexed look on his face now. "Yeah, definitely an unexpected turn that played well for us. You just never know what to expect from these people," said Tony, "but I think that you recognizing that, rolling with it and just wearing him down kept him from following through on the suicide by cop thing bro."

The two smiled and decided on where to head for lunch.

CHAPTER 13

TAKING A STEP BACK AND A STEP UP

As the sun rose over the horizon, Tony stowed away his gas mask and other equipment. Horus approached him at the back of his vehicle. The two had just concluded an early morning warrant with S.W.A.T. Over the years, it had become routine for negotiators to assist in "surround and callout" search warrants executed by the tactical team. The rationale for this was that if the search warrant started with consistent effective communication, the likelihood of compliance would be high, and if there wasn't compliance, a barricade could be declared, and the negotiation would start immediately.

The warrant had gone off without a hitch and Tony was still a little early for his shift to start. Horus cleared his throat and said, "Hey, you want to go grab a coffee?"

"Sure," replied Tony, "but it will be tea for me." The two met up at the coffee shop, and once they got their warm drinks they sat down to chat. Horus was always fidgety, but today he seemed extra anxious.

"You good man?" said Tony.

"Yeah, I just wanted to bring something up, but don't want it to be weird."

"Dude, you are making it weird now. If you're going to ask me out, just do it, I am confident in my masculinity." Horus frowned at Tony. "I am kidding man, what's on your mind?"

"Well, I want to discuss what you think about taking my position over when I am gone," said Horus. "I am planning to walk away from this in about a year."

Tony and Horus had discussed this possibility in the last couple years a few times, but now Horus was much closer to leaving the department after 30 years of service. There was much more of a serious tone this time around. Tony never really pictured himself as a team lead in that way and didn't know how he would do in permanently taking a step back from his favorite position of being a coach or being the one on a telephone. He had run the team to cover for Horus from time-to-time, but not in such a long-term capacity. The other worry Tony had was that Horus had been a tactical officer before he became a full-time negotiator, so he had a lot more clout and respect with the S.W.A.T. operators. Being selected for Horus's position would mean being stationed with the operators and having to earn their respect for the position.

Tony mentioned this to Horus who replied, "You have to be kidding. You have been doing this for five years now and have had tons of critical calls with these guys. They know you, they trust you, and you are wanted over here." Tony then mentioned that he didn't know if he would be the right fit, and Horus volleyed with the fact that Tony was already teaching all over the department and city already, which was a big part of his work week. Tony and Horus finished the conversation by discussing the positives and negatives of Horus's position at length that morning and then said their goodbyes. Before leaving Tony promised Horus he would be sure to consider their discussion and do some more fact finding about the responsibilities of the position.

Tony then drove to meet with Monica to start their day at the precinct. As they began driving around the city, he and Monica started the conversation about Horus's position. Monica had her reservations, and selfishly, she didn't want to lose Tony as her partner, but she also knew he would be great in the position and wanted to support him. It was a tough conversation. As they were about 10 minutes into the discussion a hot-call rang out of a subject inside of an apartment with his gun, claiming to be suicidal. The conversation would have to be put on hold. As the two responded they saw Derrick had also put himself enroute to the call. Tony was notorious for driving like an old man while on duty, but Derrick always gave him a hard time because any time there was a potential negotiation, "Tony finds the effing gas pedal all of a sudden." And today was no different.

Upon arriving on scene, they coordinated with patrol to surround the second story apartment, mindful of the risk posed by the suicidal subject having an elevated position, leaving the officers at a tactical disadvantage. As they were speaking with the Sergeant on scene for the basic intelligence and game plan, Monica made her way over to the caller, who was standing on the edge of the parking lot of the apartment complex. The woman, Tabytha, had called when she received a text at work from her boyfriend, who went by Biff, who was currently in the apartment.

The text had been a 'goodbye' text and detailed that Biff was planning on taking his life with either his handgun or prescription pills. Tabytha told Monica that Biff had lost his job as a delivery driver several months back and had taken to drinking a lot as of late. She also shared that Biff may have some mild depression he was dealing with just prior to the firing. Tabytha said she was trying her best to carry them through this rough patch, but Biff was making it very difficult. Just then, Tabytha's cell phone rang.

She looked at Monica with panic in her eyes, "It's him." Monica motioned calmly for Tabytha to hand her the phone and she did.

"Hey! W-w-what's going on? Why are the cops here?" slurred Biff.

"Hi, my name is Monica, I am outside your apartment here with the officers, and want to know if you'd be willing to come outside to talk?"

"Fuck no!," yelled Biff. Monica knew this was a perfect opportunity to let Biff feel empowered by letting him know it was okay to say 'no'. Tony nodded to Monica knowing they were both on the same page.

"That's fair, you know I had to ask though," replied Monica evenly.

"Well... I ain't fucking coming out f-f-f-f-for no one," stuttered Biff, almost as if he was unsure of what was happening here.

"I can respect that. I'd like to share with you why we are here," said Monica in a very warm tone.

"I don't give a shit why!," Biff barked.

"Well, you did ask me what was going on, and why the cops were here, so I would like to show you respect and answer that," Monica said.

"Oh yeah, I am sorry, I did ask that, and I am just a bit hungover from last night. I haven't slept in days," Biff said.

"Well it sounds like you might have a lot of stress going on, from what you are saying," responded Monica.

"Fuck yeah, I do, I try and try and try, but I just keep getting hit with problemsssss. I don't know, I don't know what to do, and it just keeps getting worse, and my roommate is making things harder on me, putting pressure on me and I am trying," said Biff as he started to cry.

Tony had been close enough to the phone to hear what Biff was saying so he could coach Monica. Tony then quickly stepped to where Tabytha was and said, "Who is the roommate?"

Tabytha, with an inquisitive look replied, "Roommate? We don't have a roommate. We have been together for four years. We have a dog together and have been at this apartment for two years." Tabytha looked frustrated. Tony apologized and then explained that he had probably misunderstood. As he came back, Monica was still having a good conversation with Biff. Tony updated the supervisor and officers on scene that the communication was going well, and rapport was being built. Derrick arrived and took over speaking with Tabytha.

As the conversation continued, it only became more bizarre, and it was clear that the alcohol was impairing Biff's impulse control. Amongst the topics Biff brought up with Monica were his affinity for African-American women which he had deduced Monica was, how he was unfulfilled in his sex life with his 'roommate' who Monica confirmed was apparently Tabytha (although Tabytha was unaware she was considered a roommate), and how he 'handled' the sexual frustration through 'self-soothing' tactics.

Monica kept a calm, professional and even tone throughout the entire communication, but every few minutes she gave Tony a look that communicated, "I CANNOT BELIEVE THIS GUY." Monica was always a lady in speech and in action, and very spiritual to boot, so Biff was definitely making her demonstrate her ability to be in control of her reactions.

As Biff continued for about two hours, Monica rolled with it and started to play into Biff's weakness. Biff finally relented, "I cannot wait to meet you."

Tony wrote Monica a note, "Tell him then this is a perfect opportunity for us to meet now." Monica read the note and presented the idea to Biff.

"Nah, I don't know. I can't trust what is going to happen when I get out there," he said.

Monica came back with, "Well, Biff I have to be honest with you, we have been on the phone for hours and I have to use a restroom. We either do this now, or I run to a convenience store, and pass you off to my partner."

Biff quickly responded, "No, no, no, I can't have you waiting."

"Oh, I won't be waiting, I will pass you off to my partner Tony and go use the restroom," explained Monica in a very direct way.

"Okay, okay, I don't want to talk to some other jackass out there, and I don't want you going anywhere before I can meet you," said Biff. Biff, of course, took ten minutes to get dressed and put his socks and shoes on, but he did eventually stumble down the steps of the apartment with his hands up yelling,

"Where's Monica, I am coming out to Monica!"

By the look on Tabytha's face, she was not impressed with her 'roommates' behavior. Biff was detained and after Monica kept

Taking a Step Back and a Step Up   151

her word to speak with him, Derrick transported Biff to an emergency mental health facility for an evaluation.

*   *   *

Several weeks later Tony was pumping gas into he and Monica's vehicle as they started their shift when he got a call from their Sergeant. Tony sat down in the vehicle and answered the call on speaker phone so Monica could hear the call as well.

"Hey, I need you guys to head to Southside precinct. They are working a barricade," said their Sergeant.

Monica quickly and sarcastically replied, "Good Morning to you too!" as she flashed Tony an eyebrow. Their boss had a bad habit of shot-gunning them assignments first thing in the morning without good manners, and Monica was always quick to call him out.

He then replied, "Sorry, sorry. Good morning, but yeah this guy attempted to strangle his wife, and is now refusing to come out of the house. The supervisor in that area is asking for our help."

"Sounds good sir, we will head that way," said Tony.

As they drove to the call they switched over to the South Precinct radio channel to hear the radio chatter.

"The suspect is on the line with 911 now," said the dispatcher. "He is yelling something about getting everyone back."

A sergeant at the scene got on the radio, "Okay, patch that call into me." Tony and Monica flashed each other a knowing and disapproving look from prior poor experiences.

Monica got on the radio, "We are about fifteen minutes out, can we suggest the Sergeant does NOT get on the phone, so he can run the scene, and assign that to a patrol officer?"

151

Crickets, for a moment, and then the Sergeant answered, "I agree, that is a better plan."

Monica smiled, "Good." Tony and Monica made it in under fifteen minutes to the call and went straight to the Sergeant to ask who knew most about the call.

He pointed them in the direction of an older officer on a cell phone who was pacing all over, "That's the one you are looking for, he is on the phone with the suspect." Walking behind the officer on the cell phone was a familiar face, Savannah. Savannah was a newer negotiator that Tony had helped a little as she was starting on the team. She seemed very interested in improving as a communicator and always asked a lot of questions. She looked at Tony and Monica and threw her hands up in the air. Tony walked up to see what the story was.

Savannah shared, "I am trying my best to help this officer on the phone, but he keeps walking away from me. I think it is because he thinks I am just another patrol officer since I am in my blues."

Tony nodded, "I get it, let me get him to understand what we are doing here. You are his coach."

All of a sudden, the officer on the phone turned around and yelled out indiscriminately, "He hung up on me, he is pissed." No one seemed to be paying attention.

Tony walked up to the officer, extended his hand and introduced himself, "Hey brother, I am Tony. I am one of the crisis negotiators. You are doing a good job man. What is your name?"

"Hey, I am Gabe. I kind of don't know what I am doing here, but this guy recognizes me from last week. I had to come out here for a disturbance call and he liked me, hated my partner," the officer replied as they shook hands.

"Perfect, we will want to utilize your previous rapport with him and keep you on the line if that is okay," said Tony. "This is Savannah, she is one of our very capable negotiators. I am going to have her coach you. She will help you navigate the conversation with this guy, but first I am going to put you in a cool vehicle, with speakerphone and out of line of sight from the suspect's residence to keep you both safe," added Tony.

Gabe gave a look of relief and Tony walked him over to their Tahoe. Once Tony had Savannah seated in the front passenger seat of the Tahoe and Gabe situated in the driver seat, he told Gabe, "Let's get back on the line."

"I told you, just everyone leave and I'll be fine," said Mr. Liu over the Tahoe's Bluetooth system.

Gabe started to reply, "But Mr. Liu..."

Just then Gabe was sharply cut-off by Mr. Liu, "You don't tell me what to do. My wife started this today, and she didn't like how it was going to end so now she called you. I will not let myself be taken advantage of or let anyone tell me how to run my house."

Gabe looked at Savannah, who looked over to Tony as the call ended.

Tony cleared over the radio, "Negotiations to command, we are off-line." The Sergeant acknowledged.

Tony then turned to Gabe, "Gabe, what do you hear?"

"He sounds pissed," replied Gabe.

Tony nodded, "What else do you hear?" Gabe seemed to ponder. Tony stayed silent.

"Well, it seems like he is really mad at his wife and now he sees us as her tool," said Gabe.

"Excellent man. So, tell him you hear that. And next, ask him how it got this way. Cause we have to prove to him that we are here to help him, without telling him we are here to help him."

Tony then winked at Savannah, and mouthed, "You got this."

Gabe then got back on the line with Mr. Liu. As he started with the suggested paraphrase, Mr. Liu seemed thrown off. "You aren't taking her side?" he said in a surprised tone.

Savannah then wrote on the small white board that Tony had handed her, "There are two sides to a story, and I am here to listen to yours." Gabe quickly caught on to the notes.

"Hey Mr. Liu, just like the last time I was here. I don't make decisions based on one person's version of the events, I am here to listen to your side too."

From that point on Gabe re-connected with Mr. Liu. There were of course ups and downs during the exchange, but the system was working. As the system was working, Tony found himself trusting Savannah to coach and only giving her input sparingly. He focused on listening, getting on the radio to give updates to the supervisor on scene as to the progress of communication, and sharing intelligence that Monica was working on to Savannah. Tony was running the team, and he felt pretty good actually.

As the negotiation entered its second hour, Mr. Liu appeared to be growing tired. The team suspected he might be under the influence of alcohol or drugs at 10 in the morning, a suspicion later confirmed. While Gabe and Savannah pressed on, Tony reminded them that patience would ultimately pay off and encouraged them for their efforts. When Mr. Liu mentioned needing to use the restroom, a distinctive sound, unmistakable to most police officers, echoed in the background.

It sounded as if Mr. Liu was unloading bullets from the magazine of a gun and they were landing on a glass top table. This matched the intelligence from officers to the rear of the home who had reported that Mr. Liu was in the backyard a short time ago, sitting at a patio table. They had not mentioned a gun. Tony cleared over the radio to let officers know what was going on. The officers to the rear of the residence confirmed, Mr. Liu was in the backyard with the gun. There were rounds on the table, but he had the gun at the bottom of his chin.

The line had been silent for a moment, and Tony whispered to Savannah, "Let's address the gun."

Gabe heard the message and didn't require a note, "Mr. Liu, what are you doing?"

Gabe went to say something else, and Savannah stopped him with a light grip on his bicep, giving him the signal to let the question work. About 20 seconds passed and Mr. Liu eventually said, "Don't worry about me Gabe."

This was concerning.

As Tony was clearing on the radio warning of the risk of suicide, Savannah wrote on the whiteboard, "Ask him what he is doing with the gun."

Gabe nodded and said, "Mr. Liu, how is holding that weapon going to help you?" Mr. Liu sighed heavily and stayed quiet.

Tony whispered to Savannah, and she then wrote on the board, "How can you expect us to leave with you in this place?" Gabe put his twist on the words and delivered.

Mr. Liu seemed to come out of the darkness, "I know, you are just trying to help me."

Savannah patted Gabe on the shoulder with a smile. "I am Mr. Liu, so can you come out now?"

Mr. Liu, defeated, said, "Yes, but I need to use the bathroom," and hung up the phone.

Tony let everyone on scene know that they were off-line and that the subject was claiming to be using the restroom before coming out.

He then turned his attention to Gabe and Savannah, "Great job guys."

Gabe, who was sweating even though they were in an air-conditioned Tahoe, said, "This is freaking exhausting. You guys do this all the time?" Savannah nodded her head.

Gabe shook his head, chuckled and said, "Thank you for helping me. Both of you."

Tony then said, "Real quick, before we get on the phone, that 'yes' is going to be nothing without a plan. We have to walk him through a detailed visual of what this is going to look like. So, when you get back on, ask how he's feeling, then ask him to tell you what it looks like to him to come out. Then walk him through what it actually will look like." Savannah and Gabe nodded and made the call.

As Gabe reconnected with Mr. Liu the quick nurture of asking how he was landed just as it needed to, and Mr. Liu talked about his anxiety. After Gabe listened and worked through the fear and anxiety, they moved into talking about what coming out looked like. From the discussion it was clear that the 'yes' Mr. Liu gave was intended as a time buyer for him. When Gabe brought him back to the topic, Mr. Liu did something surprising. He started to insult Gabe and say quite a few nasty things to him. Tony knew from past negotiations that this was the alcohol talking and something else. Tony was certain that before he came out, Mr. Liu was testing Gabe. He was trying to see if Gabe was really here to help him or if he would turn into a badge heavy cop the moment he pressed him.

Recognizing the danger of losing the entire negotiation Tony quickly broke protocol by waving to Gabe and whispering to him directly, "Don't take the bait. Just stay silent." Gabe did, and Tony turned to Savannah to apologize for talking to the primary. The silence hung heavy, and Mr. Liu filled it.

"What? You aren't man enough to answer me?" Gabe and Savannah were on the same page of staying silent.

After about another 10 seconds Savannah had Gabe tell Mr. Liu, "You just sounded pretty upset and like you really wanted to get that all out."

Mr. Liu replied, "Yeah, I guess I am just mad at myself. Okay, I am walking out now with nothing in my hands." Tony was already on the radio letting everyone know to expect the front door. Mr. Liu came out and was taken into custody.

After the call Tony made sure to thank the Sergeant for his patience and willingness to work together. In the debrief he also praised both Gabe and Savannah heavily for their patience, teamwork, and empathetic approach to Mr. Liu's situation. As Tony and Monica were leaving the scene Gabe walked up and thanked Tony. Tony made sure to remind Gabe that he had done the work, even before they got there by treating Mr. Liu with respect on the previous contact which made Gabe invaluable that day. Tony also told Gabe that he appreciated the fact that he constantly reinforced the idea to Mr. Liu that he was there to help him and wasn't going to give up.

"Interested in negotiations, Gabe?" asked Tony.

"Nah, this is enough of an experience for me," smiled Gabe.

"Well keep it in mind, and reach out if you ever change your mind," said Tony. Gabe and Tony shook hands and exchanged smiles as they parted ways.

Savannah walked up shortly after. "Tony, thank you for your help, I couldn't have done it without you."

Tony replied, "Yes, you could have," with a smile.

"Well, I felt fully supported there and it felt really good to coach someone to a positive resolution. It is a different side of things," said Savannah.

Tony continued to smile and said, "You did great. Proud of you and see you on the next one 'coach.'"

As Tony was sitting at home later that evening on his couch working on some schoolwork, he started daydreaming about the call from earlier that day. Tony took a sip from his London fog latte as he reflected, and a smile crept onto his face as he ran the events of the call through his head. Thinking about what he had taken away from that day Tony had to admit to himself that being patient was more complex from the position of a team lead, a different kind of fortitude.

Most importantly, Tony realized that demonstrating trust in the team members brought the best out in them, and he would continue to work on nurturing that as he progressed. Over the years on the negotiation team, Tony had played a role in instructing and training most of the negotiators in some capacity. He appreciated that it was time to trust that he had trained them well and let the team members shine as he supported and guided them.

Tony had gone through so many stages in his career and his journey as a police communicator was now taking him somewhere new and exciting. Every twist and turn was meant to be and this would be a new chapter to take head on.

At that moment Tony recognized he was prepared to help run the team more permanently, and like Savannah had said earlier that day, "It's a different side of things."

As Tony envisioned what the future would look like, he also thought to himself that building relationships within the team and in the department would play a big role in the team's future, and the future of the program. He knew he had a lot to learn, and it would be hard work, but Tony was ready for the new challenge to keep sharing what he had learned with others who also wanted to excel and bring more people hope.

AUTHOR BIO

Lorenzo 'Enzo' Ortiz is a Crisis Negotiations team lead in one of the largest cities in the U.S. Enzo has a Master's Degree in Education, A Bachelor's Degree in Psychology and is currently working towards a Master's Degree in Clinical Mental Health.

As a lifelong student of the art, music and science of communication, Enzo found a niche in law enforcement where he was able to learn, practice and hone these skills in some of the most intense moments of other people's lives. Enzo carries and shares 19 years of effective law enforcement communications experience with people on a daily basis as he instructs about crisis intervention and crisis negotiation with hundreds of police officers a year. Enzo has been the recipient of multiple awards and commendations associated with his application of these skills and wants to share these skills with you.